LEOPARD AT THE LODGE

They had just been watching a warthog splashing through the shallows, when Mandy suddenly stiffened, alerted by a slender moving object hanging down from the branch of a tree a little way beyond the perimeter fence. Panning upwards with the binoculars, she saw an animal lying along the branch, a lean and powerful silhouette, stretched out full length and so well camouflaged that it was almost invisible. Only the constantly moving tail had given away its hiding place.

She tugged at James's sleeve. 'Look there. In that tree! I think it's . . . It *is*! It's a leopard!' She let out her breath in a long sigh. 'Oh, it's beautiful.'

Please look this way, she begged silently. As if it could hear her, the leopard turned its wedge-shaped head. Mandy watched, spellbound.

Animal Ark series

1 Kittens in the Kitchen
2 Pony in the Porch
3 Puppies in the Pantry
4 Goat in the Garden
5 Hedgehogs in the Hall
6 Badger in the Basement
7 Cub in the Cupboard
8 Piglet in a Playpen
9 Owl in the Office
10 Lamb in the Laundry
11 Bunnies in the Bathroom
12 Donkey on the Doorstep
13 Hamster in a Hamper
14 Goose on the Loose
15 Calf in the Cottage
16 Koalas in a Crisis
17 Wombat in the Wild
18 Roo on the Rock
19 Squirrels in the School
20 Guinea-pig in the Garage
21 Fawn in the Forest
22 Shetland in the Shed
23 Swan in the Swim
24 Lion by the Lake
25 Elephants in the East
26 Monkeys on the Mountain
27 Dog at the Door
28 Foals in the Field

29 Sheep at the Show
30 Racoons on the Roof
31 Dolphin in the Deep
32 Bears in the Barn
33 Otter in the Outhouse
34 Whale in the Waves
35 Hound at the Hospital
36 Rabbits on the Run
37 Horse in the House
38 Panda in the Park
39 Tiger on the Track
40 Gorilla in the Glade
41 Tabby in the Tub
42 Chinchilla up the Chimney
43 Puppy in a Puddle
44 Leopard at the Lodge
Hauntings 1: Dog in the Dungeon
Hauntings 2: Cat in the Crypt
Hauntings 3: Stallion in the Storm
Ponies at the Point
Seal on the Shore
Pigs at the Picnic
Sheepdog in the Snow
Kitten in the Cold
Fox in the Frost
Hamster in the Holly
Pony in the Post
Animal Ark Favourites

LUCY DANIELS

Leopard
— at the —
Lodge

Illustrations by Ann Baum

**Hodder
Children's
Books**

a division of Hodder Headline plc

Special thanks to Susan Bentley
Thanks also to C. J. Hall, B.Vet.Med., M.R.C.V.S., for reviewing
the veterinary information contained in this book.

Animal Ark is a trademark of Working Partners Limited
Text copyright © 2000 Working Partners Limited
Created by Working Partners Limited, London W6 OQT
Original series created by Ben M. Baglio
Illustrations copyright © 2000 Ann Baum

First published in Great Britain in 2000
by Hodder Children's Books

A Catalogue record for this book is available from the British Library

ISBN 0 340 77843 1

Typeset by Avon Dataset Ltd, Bidford-on-Avon, Warks

Printed and bound in Great Britain by
Clays Ltd, St Ives plc

Hodder Children's Books
a division of Hodder Headline plc
338 Euston Road
London NW1 3BH

One

'I've got my binoculars ready! Roll out the elephants, lions, water buffalo, sweeping herds of wildebeest...' Adam Hope enthused as he admired the dam that stretched into the distance below the Ubungane Lodge resort.

'You'll be lucky, Dad!' Mandy said with a grin, shading her eyes against the orange glare on the water. It was late afternoon and they had just arrived at the resort which was part of a huge nature reserve in South Africa. 'Even here you wouldn't see all those animals at the same time!'

'Oh, I don't know! Remember what Levina

says,' her dad replied. ' "In Africa nothing is as you expect it!" '

Mandy Hope's mum and dad ran a busy veterinary practice in Yorkshire. They were here to visit their friend Dr Levina Lemiso, who was working at a research base attached to Ubungane Lodge. Levina had suggested they stay at the resort, which was owned by her friends, Pam and Tony McKenzie.

Mandy grinned at her best friend, James Hunter, who was spending the Easter holidays with them in South Africa. James was eleven and in the class below her at school. 'Dad's got a point,' she told him, pushing her hair back off her face. 'It's supposed to be winter here and it's much hotter than our summer!'

'Which is why I'm going to head straight for the pool, the minute we get unpacked,' Mr Hope declared. 'I'm determined to squeeze in a swim before the sun disappears for the night!'

'Hmm.' Mandy's blue eyes widened innocently. 'Going to do an impression of your favourite animal – a hippo?'

'Cheeky!' Mr Hope swatted his daughter playfully with his baseball cap. James burst out laughing as Mandy leaped nimbly out of the way.

'Right, everyone,' Emily Hope said, appearing at the door of the resort reception. 'David here is going to show us to our cabins. He's helped out at the resort since he was little, so he knows everything there is to know!'

Mandy saw that David had fair hair and tanned skin. She already knew that the McKenzies had two children: David, who was thirteen, and Sophie, who was nine.

'No tents this time!' Mandy said to James. When they had visited Levina in the Congo and Kenya they had camped outside the research bases, but this trip was going to be more luxurious. Mandy was thrilled to be back in Africa.

'Hi,' David McKenzie greeted them. 'Welcome to Ubungane Lodge! Come this way, please.'

'Hi.' Mandy and James gathered up their bags and followed him across the neatly-mown lawns of the resort.

'Levina left a message to say she'll come over and see us this evening,' Mrs Hope told them. 'Apparently she's gone out to check up on a young leopard. She thinks he's lost his electronic tag.'

'Oh,' Mandy said, thrilled at the thought of having leopards so close, but concerned for the cub. 'I hope there's nothing wrong.'

'I'm sure the leopard's fine,' her mum reassured her. 'It's not that unusual for these tags to come loose.'

'Your mum's right,' Mr Hope agreed. 'Don't let that imagination of yours work overtime, Mandy. We're here for a holiday, remember?'

Mandy grinned, glancing sideways at her dad, who was already looking relaxed in his jungle-print shirt over baggy shorts.

'All the cabins are named after different animals,' David explained, as they passed a group of wooden grass-roofed cabins. 'Mr and Mrs Hope, you're in Gazelle Lodge. And Mandy and James, you're in Leela's Lodge.'

'Well!' Mr Hope rubbed his dark beard. 'I don't think I've ever heard of a "Leela"!'

'Oh, Dad!' Mandy rolled her eyes, used to her dad's terrible jokes.

David grinned. 'Leela's a leopard Sandie Howard hand-reared from an orphaned cub at the research base. She's been introduced back into the wild now.'

'Sandie Howard's a big cat expert, isn't she?' James said. 'I read an article she wrote in a wildlife magazine.'

'That's right. She's a bit of a celebrity around

here,' David told them. 'She worked at the base for about eight years. That's where Leela lived in her *boma* until she learned to hunt for herself.'

'*Boma*?' Mandy queried. 'I thought that was the word for a village.'

'It is,' David explained. 'But it has other meanings, like "enclosure" or even "tourist rest area" nowadays. Sandie's working down south at the moment, but she visits now and again to check that Leela's OK.'

Sandie must be thrilled to see the leopard she has hand-reared living free, Mandy thought. It wasn't always possible to re-introduce animals into the wild once they were used to being around humans.

'How near to the resort does Leela come?' James asked. They had reached their cabins now. She saw that Gazelle Lodge and Leela's Lodge were next to each other.

David smiled. 'You might see her through binoculars if you're lucky. But if she did come here, she wouldn't be able to get inside the perimeter fence. Only non-dangerous animals are allowed to wander about freely.'

'Phew!' Mr Hope said. 'I wouldn't fancy coming face to face with a leopard or a lion on my way to breakfast!'

David ran his hand through his short fair hair and laughed. 'No chance of that, Mr Hope. You might have noticed the armed guards on your way through the main gates. Around here we say, "a leopard is a leopard".'

'Meaning they're unpredictable and incredibly dangerous?' Emily Hope added.

David nodded. 'No one but Sandie would risk getting close to Leela, especially now that she has two cubs.'

'Cubs?' Mandy asked, excitedly. It would be wonderful to catch a glimpse of Leela and her cubs!

'Well – I'll leave you to settle in,' David said, once he had shown them their accommodation. 'You'll find some complimentary cold drinks inside your cabin.'

A few minutes later, Mandy and James were studying the photos that decorated their cabin's walls while they drank glasses of sweet mango juice.

'Oh, aren't these gorgeous?' Mandy exclaimed, reading the inscription beneath one of the photos. ' "Leela at three months old – still with her baby fluff." '

In a later photograph, a deeply-tanned woman was dragging something on a string, while the leopard chased it. 'Look at this one,' James said. ' "Sandie playing with Leela – 13 months." I wonder how old Leela was when Sandie released her into the wild?'

'Maybe David knows. We can ask him later.' Mandy drained her glass, then gestured towards the screens of plaited grass that separated the two sleeping areas. Mosquito nets were looped neatly above the beds. 'Where do you want to sleep, James?'

'I don't mind,' he replied absent-mindedly, fishing about in his hold-all. 'Ah, got it.' He pulled out his camera, then went over to the window and peered out. 'I should be able to get some great shots with this new lens.'

Mandy left her unpacking and joined him at the window. Their lodge was on a hill and they could see over and beyond the perimeter fence. A family of giraffes had come down to the dam to drink. They spread their long legs, dipping their necks forward to reach the water. It was a peaceful scene.

'Isn't it beautiful here?' Mandy sighed. 'I'm really looking forward to seeing Levina again.'

'Me too.' James checked his watch. 'Wow! We've only got about an hour or so before dinner.'

The first afternoon of their holiday was slipping away already. Mandy glanced at her open suitcase. 'Let's unpack later and not waste any more time!'

Mandy heard splashing sounds as they approached the swimming-pool. Mr Hope was ploughing through the water, head turned to one side as he gulped in air. Water was spraying in all directions.

'Your dad's not exactly a smooth swimmer, is he?' James commented.

Mandy's lips trembled with laughter. 'Mum says he's an enthusiastic swimmer – rather than an efficient one.'

Suddenly, a small brownish animal shot out of the bushes, right in front of her. It was roundish with a pointed face and small ears and looked rather like a large guinea-pig. Lifting its head, it glanced curiously at Mandy and James, then launched itself straight into the pool.

'I think that's a hyrax,' Mandy said. She had seen them before, living on rocky hillsides, their natural habitat. But what was this one doing diving into a swimming-pool?

'Uh oh!' James gasped.

They watched, open-mouthed, as the little animal swam straight towards Adam Hope. Mr Hope had turned over on to his back and was now floating, eyes closed, blissfully unaware that he was no longer alone.

'Dad!' Mandy called. 'Look out!'

It was too late. The small wet creature scrambled out of the water and up on to the human raft. Mr Hope let out a yell. His hands clutched at empty air and he sagged in the middle.

'I can't bear to look!' James covered his eyes as man and hyrax sank in a froth of bubbles.

A blonde girl dashed up to the side of the pool. 'Oh, no!' she cried, looking horrified, as the little animal bobbed to the surface a second or two before Mr Hope reappeared. 'Dilly – come here!'

Mandy noticed that the girl bore a strong resemblance to David McKenzie, and guessed that this must be his sister, Sophie.

'Is Dilly yours?' Mandy asked, rather surprised. She had never heard of anyone keeping a hyrax as a pet.

The girl nodded, biting her lip and looking rather embarrassed at her pet's behaviour. 'I'm really sorry, but she's used to getting in the pool with me. Dilly! Come here!'

The hyrax's ears pricked up at the sound of her owner's voice. Now that her 'raft' had sunk, the little animal began doggy-paddling back to the side of the pool. Her wedge-shaped nose stuck out of the water and she blinked up happily at her audience.

'Ugh!' Mr Hope had found his feet, wet hair streaming over his face. 'What on earth was that?'

'A hyrax called Dilly! Are you OK, Dad?' Mandy was trying hard not to laugh.

'I'm really sorry!' the girl called out. 'Dilly wouldn't have hurt you.'

She kneeled down and scooped up the little animal. 'Naughty girl!' she scolded, cuddling her. 'You mustn't go for water rides on the guests!'

Mandy and James took another look at Mr Hope's surprised face and burst out laughing. 'Sorry, Dad! 'Mandy gasped. 'You did ask for company!'

Adam Hope grinned. 'I suppose I did! Oh, well – no harm done.' He turned round and headed for the deep end.

'You're David's sister Sophie, aren't you?' Mandy asked.

Sophie nodded. 'And you're Mandy and James. David told me about you.' By now Dilly had climbed up and draped herself round the girl's neck.

Mandy had only seen hyraxes from a distance until now. Close up, the white crescent-shaped markings above each eye gave Dilly a wide-awake appearance. 'She's lovely, isn't she?' Mandy said admiringly. 'Can we touch her?'

Sophie nodded, obviously pleased to show off her pet. Mandy and James stroked Dilly, who began grinding her teeth.

'Why's she doing that?' James asked, sounding worried. 'Will she bite?'

'No. It means she's happy.' Sophie grinned proudly. 'Would you like to come and see the other animals? David and Lindiwe have got pets as well. Lindiwe's our friend. Her mum works in the hotel office and her dad's the manager at the base.'

'We'd love to, wouldn't we, James?' Mandy said at once.

James nodded. 'But I think that might have to wait. Here's your mum . . .'

'I've just been to call for you,' Mrs Hope said, smiling. She was wearing a long-sleeved cotton dress, and had pinned up her long auburn hair. 'Hello, you must be Sophie. Is that a hyrax?'

'No, it's an Olympic swimmer!' Mandy joked.

Mrs Hope chuckled when she heard how her husband's swim had been interrupted. 'We've been invited to join the other guests for a *braai*. Levina's on her way over here to meet us for dinner.'

'A *braai*? Great,' James said. 'I'm starving.' Mandy and James had enjoyed the local version of a barbecue on their previous trips to Africa.

Mandy grinned. 'You're always starving!'

'I'll just put Dilly away for the night,' Sophie said. 'See you at the *braai*.' She walked off with the hyrax still draped round her neck like a wet, furry scarf.

'See you later,' Mandy called after her.

She turned back to her mum, who was watching her husband enjoying his swim. 'I think we might have trouble getting Dad out of the pool.'

Mrs Hope's eyes sparkled. 'No problem, when you know how.' She walked to the edge of the pool. 'Adam!' she called. 'Food!'

'Come and eat!' A tanned, fair-haired man was waving a pair of cooking tongs.

'That's Tony McKenzie, David and Sophie's dad,' Mrs Hope told Mandy and James.

Appetising smells rose from the *braai* where Mr McKenzie was waiting for them. 'Chicken kebabs. Sausages. Salads. Plenty for everyone!' Apparently someone had told him that Mandy was a vegetarian. He placed a mysterious looking package wrapped in leaves on her plate. 'Careful how you unwrap it,' he told her. 'It's very hot.'

Once James had helped himself from the barbecue, they carried their food over to where Levina was already sitting next to Mandy's mum and dad.

'Mandy! James! How lovely to see you both

again,' Levina cried, standing up to give them both a hug. She was a slight figure in her yellow and blue robe, and matching turban. She had been born in Tanzania, but she had studied in England for a time with Mandy's parents. Now she had returned to Africa to study wildlife.

'Is the young male leopard all right, Levina?' Mandy asked her friend eagerly. 'Only Mum said you were late back because his radio tag had come off . . .'

Levina smiled. 'You haven't changed, Mandy! Animals always come first with you, don't they? The leopard's fine. We fitted another tag.'

'Oh, that's good.' Mandy unwrapped the parcel of leaves to reveal a pile of roasted vegetables.

The restaurant was full of guests enjoying their meal. Lanterns hanging from the trees cast a warm glow over the wooden tables and chairs. The scent of huge pink flowers on a nearby bush hung on the night air.

'So – tell me, what have you all been doing since we last met?' Levina asked.

Emily Hope grinned. 'The usual things; setting broken limbs, attending calvings.'

'Who's looking after Animal Ark while you're away?' Levina wanted to know.

'We've got a stand-in vet, Alistair King. He's helped us out before,' Mr Hope told her. 'And Simon, our nurse, is there too. Welford's animals are in safe hands. But how about you, Levina – what are you working on at the moment?'

Levina's dark eyes sparkled. 'It's a new project that involves trailing around in the bush downwind of a herd of *Hippotragus equinus* – roan antelope!'

Mandy had seen roan antelope on previous visits to Africa and thought them very handsome with their backward-curving horns and stiff, horse-like manes.

'Is the project going well?' Mrs Hope asked.

'Yes, very well.' Levina spoke in a low, musical voice. 'The only problem is, I'll have to be away from the base for a few days. I had hoped to be spending that time with you.'

Mandy guessed that her parents would be disappointed, but her mum smiled. 'It can't be helped. We'll still have plenty of time left when you get back.'

'That's right.' Adam Hope attempted to look mournful. 'I expect we'll just have to put up with sunbathing, reading and generally having a good rest.'

Levina gave a relieved laugh. 'Thanks. I've been feeling really guilty. It's not exactly hospitable, is it? I invite you out here, then disappear off into the bush!'

Mandy felt a bit disappointed, but then she had a sudden thought. Maybe Levina would need some help with her project. But before she had a chance to offer, Levina turned to her and said, 'I've just heard something that might interest you. Sandie Howard's on her way to the base.'

Mandy exchanged glances with James. If Sandie Howard was visiting, Mandy realised, she probably wanted to check up on Leela and her cubs.

'Great!' James said. 'We can ask Sandie about Leela. And she knows about black panthers too. She mentioned them in that magazine article I read.' Mandy remembered James showing her the magazine on the plane. 'Black panthers are really rare in southern Africa, aren't they?' he said enthusiastically. 'Wouldn't it be brilliant to see one? Maybe we could ask Sandie Howard about it. I bet she knows everything about big cats.'

'Ah.' Levina gave them a warm smile. 'Somehow, I don't think I'm going to be missed too much!'

Two

Mandy was woken by strange barking noises. For a moment she couldn't think where she was. Then she looked up, saw the grass roof of the cabin and smelled the rich scents of early morning.

Africa! She leaped out of bed and went over to the window. Pulling back the blind, she saw that the shores of the dam were still wreathed in mist. Huge silhouettes of elephants stood in the water, shadowy and mysterious. It was a magical scene.

The noises outside the cabin came again, louder this time. Mandy could hear scuffles, growls and barks. Hurriedly, she pulled on a pair of shorts and a T-shirt.

James stuck his head round the grass screen, blinking sleepily through his glasses. 'What's that? It sounds like a fight.'

'Or something being attacked,' Mandy said, worried. 'I was about to go and investigate.'

'Maybe we ought to wake your mum and dad,' James suggested.

Mandy nodded. 'Let's see what's going on first.'

She caught sight of the culprits as soon as she opened the cabin door. Darting in and out of the bushes were two reddish creatures, about the size of domestic dogs. They had dark saddle markings along their backs and black stripes down the length of their tails.

'I think they're some kind of jackal,' Mandy whispered, as she and James hung back warily.

'I think you're right. Are they dangerous?' James asked.

One of the animals was crouched beside the bush, waiting for the other to reappear from inside the thicket. The moment it stepped out, the first animal leaped on it. Snapping and gripping each other's necks, they rolled to the ground.

Mandy shook her head. 'I don't think so. Look – now the first one's hiding in the bushes. I think they're just playing!'

'That's right,' came a soft voice with an American accent from behind them. 'But you're wise to keep your distance until you're absolutely sure – especially with jackals.'

'Oh.' Mandy spun round. She had been too engrossed to notice anyone approaching.

The speaker was a slim woman wearing khaki shorts and a matching shirt. Her short dark hair was streaked with grey and her skin was tanned a deep caramel colour. Mandy recognised her at once from the photos in Leela's Lodge. It was Sandie Howard!

'Hi,' Mandy introduced herself. 'I'm Mandy Hope. And this is James Hunter.'

'We're here on holiday,' James explained. 'We're staying in Leela's Lodge.'

'Pleased to meet you,' the woman said. 'My name's Sandie Howard. I'm staying here too, in Elephant Lodge. I'm working at the research centre. Call me Sandie. Everyone does.'

'OK,' Mandy replied, delighted to find her so friendly.

'You two seem pretty clued up about animals,' Sandie went on.

'We've been to Africa before,' Mandy told her. 'And my parents are vets.'

James nodded.

Just then, the jackals started to growl again, apparently undeterred by their audience. One of them was crouching down now, its nose almost touching its front paws and its tail wagging, inviting its companion to chase it.

'Would it be OK if we moved a bit closer to them?' Mandy asked in a hushed voice.

Sandie nodded. 'If we're careful and don't make any sudden movements,' she replied.

Mandy laughed at the game. The jackals were fascinating. But then something startled them and they darted away. She watched them lope off into the distance. Gradually they were swallowed up by the landscape, their colouring blending in perfectly with the reddish earth.

As they strolled back towards the cabins with Sandie, they met Mandy's mum and dad. Mandy hurried over to meet them. 'Didn't you hear the jackals? You've missed all the excitement now.'

Adam Hope smiled and raised his dark eyebrows above his sunglasses. 'I think I can live without any animal incidents, just for a few weeks!'

'Mum, Dad, this is Sandie Howard,' Mandy said eagerly. 'She's just been telling us about jackals!'

'Pleased to meet you, Sandie. I hope you realise that you've made two friends for life here,' said Mr Hope.

Sandie smiled. 'Fine by me. I think it's great that Mandy and James are so interested in animals.'

'We're just off to breakfast,' Emily said. 'Would you like to join us?'

'I'd better not, but thanks,' Sandie said. 'I was just on my way to the research base when I bumped into these two. Sipho Ngomane, the manager of the base, is expecting me to arrive early.'

Mandy tried to hide her disappointment. She longed to ask Sandie about Leela.

As if Sandie had read her mind, she said, 'Why don't you all come over to the base with me? You might find it interesting to see how we track the leopards. The staff all know me, I'm sure they won't mind.'

'Can we go, Mum?' Mandy pleaded. 'We're really not hungry yet, are we, James?'

James looked doubtful. 'Er . . . no,' he said.

Emily Hope chuckled at the look on James's face. 'All right. I've got some fruit in the hut. We'll eat that on the way over.'

* * *

The base was a long wooden building with a grass roof. It had a veranda along one side, with wooden tables and benches. A number of outbuildings were clustered next to a sturdy-looking wire enclosure. Mandy wondered if that was Leela's old *boma*.

'Sandie!' A tall, friendly-looking man greeted them at the door. 'Welcome. It's good to see you again,' he said warmly.

'Sipho. Let me introduce Adam and Emily Hope,' Sandie said. 'This is Mandy, their daughter, and her friend James. Meet Sipho Ngomane, my good friend and colleague.'

The base manager was the tallest man Mandy had ever seen. He wore a beige short-sleeved shirt and baggy shorts. 'Ah, you are Levina's friends? Welcome, welcome,' he said, smiling. 'I hear you've had some adventures together in Africa before. Levina told me you took a lion cub back to join his family in the Ruwenzori mountains. Just you and a boy of the Masai. It was well done.'

'Did you?' Sandie looked impressed.

Mandy nodded. 'We had to do it, didn't we, James? The cub was lost and some farmers wanted to shoot him, in case he killed their cattle,' she explained.

James was blushing and fiddling with his glasses.

Sandie smiled at them both. 'It sounds pretty brave to me.'

Mr Hope grinned. 'When you get to know these two better, Sandie, you'll realise that they'd do anything to save an animal in trouble!'

Sipho Ngomane laughed. 'Come inside, everyone.' He led them into a large room, cooled by ceiling fans and lined with shelves of books.

'Has Levina left already?' Emily Hope asked, sitting down on a low sofa.

Sipho nodded and smiled. 'The day starts very early in Africa.'

A girl of about thirteen appeared from a side room. Sipho put his hand on her shoulder.

'Ah, Lindiwe, meet Mandy and James. Mandy and James, meet my daughter.'

Lindiwe Ngomane wore a T-shirt and shorts. She had the same slim build as her father and her dark hair curled closely round her head.

'Hi.' Lindiwe's smile lit up her whole face.

'I thought you might show Mandy and James how we track the leopards here at the reserve,' Sandie told Sipho.

'Of course,' the base manager replied. 'I'd be pleased to.' He led them into an office off the main room and took a seat near the radio. 'I expect you'd like to know where Leela and her cubs are?'

Sandie nodded, and Mandy and James exchanged enthusiastic looks. On their last trip to Africa they had seen Levina use similar radios to track tagged animals. Sipho showed them a chart that listed the frequencies of the different reserve leopards. He explained that the signals, picked up from the electronic tags, would allow him to find Leela's exact position. He pressed some buttons and the radio whined and crackled as he searched for the right frequency.

After a few moments, Mandy heard a steady blip, blip noise. 'Is that Leela?' she asked excitedly.

'No. That's a big male called Tommy. I haven't picked up Leela's frequency yet.' Sipho tried again. After more crackling and a fuzz of static, Mandy heard another sound, a regular bleep, bleep.

'Leela!' Sipho smiled. 'Her radio tag's working fine. She's just here . . .' He got up and walked over to a wall map. Different coloured marker pins were used for the signals from each leopard.

Mandy saw that Tommy's pins were blue. Leela's were red. There were yellow, black, and white pins marking the movements of the other reserve leopards.

Sipho stuck two more red pins into the map. 'This map covers about 50 square kilometres of the northern part of the reserve,' he told them.

'It's good leopard country up there,' Sandie explained. 'Mostly dry scrub and rocks. Tourists tend not to visit the area too much.' She pointed out a narrow stretch of river. 'A lot of animals gather to drink here, so Leela has a good supply of food and there are plenty of places to make a lair. She's been in the same region for the last few weeks.'

'Is that because she can't go far away from her cubs when she hunts?' Mandy asked.

Sandie nodded. 'She's probably changing dens every two to four days at the moment.'

'Why would she do that?' James wanted to know.

'The first few weeks are a dangerous time for cubs,' Sandie told him. 'Changing her den helps to throw any predators off track.'

Mandy shivered at the thought of the tiny, vulnerable cubs being stalked by predators. She knew that many cubs died in their first few weeks of life. It couldn't be easy for Leela to protect them. 'How does Leela know what to do if she hasn't got the memories of how her own mother cared for her?' she asked.

'The mothering instinct is very strong, remember,' Sipho reassured her. 'And Leela has adapted very well to the wild.'

Sandie nodded. 'Leela's healthy and strong. I don't expect her to have any problems rearing her cubs. She's clever enough to avoid trouble.'

'But leopards don't have many predators, do they?' Mandy knew it would take a powerful creature to challenge a full-grown leopard.

'Lions will kill a cub if it's out in the open,' Sandie informed her. 'They won't tolerate intruders on their territory. Leopards kill lion cubs too.'

'What about baboons?' asked James. 'You mentioned them in an article I read.'

'Yes, she'd definitely avoid those as well,' Sandie agreed. 'A troop of baboons could tear a leopard cub to pieces in minutes.'

Mandy imagined Leela deep inside the safety of a cave lair, protecting her cubs from danger.

Sandie was studying the map.

'Are you planning to go out and check on her?'
Sipho asked.

'Yes. In a day or so,' Sandie replied. She turned
to the others. 'How would you like to come with
me?'

Mandy could hardly believe her ears. A chance
to go out watching leopards with Sandie Howard!

'Yes, please!' she exclaimed. 'That would be
great, wouldn't it, James?'

'Brilliant,' James agreed, his eyes shining.

Sandie smiled. 'Well – from what I hear, you're
pretty experienced around animals. A couple of
extra pairs of eyes would be useful. And I'd be
delighted to have two vets along on the trip,' she
added, turning to Mr and Mrs Hope.

Emily and Adam Hope looked at each other
while Mandy held her breath. They *had* to agree.
In her imagination, she could see herself sitting
next to Sandie, travelling across a vast flat plane
full of every kind of South African wildlife.

At last, Mr Hope grinned, putting her out of
her misery. 'We'd love to come. Thanks, Sandie.'

That afternoon, Mandy's thoughts were occupied
with Leela and her cubs. She was longing to
go straight out and find them. The day after

tomorrow! It seemed like weeks away.

But for now she and James had to content themselves with the animals around the lodge. The high ground of the resort gave them a clear vantage point over the dam which stretched out below them.

They had just been watching a warthog splashing through the shallows, when Mandy suddenly stiffened, alerted by a slender moving object hanging down from the branch of a tree a little way beyond the perimeter fence. Panning upwards with the binoculars, she saw an animal lying along the branch, a lean and powerful silhouette, stretched out full length and so well camouflaged that it was almost invisible. Only the constantly moving tail had given away its hiding place.

She tugged at James's sleeve. 'Look there. In that tree! I think it's . . . It *is*! It's a leopard!' She let out her breath in a long sigh. 'Oh, it's beautiful.'

Please look this way, she begged silently. As if it could hear her, the leopard turned its wedge-shaped head. Mandy watched spellbound. The camouflage was perfect, the spots blending with the dappled light through the leaves.

'Have you got it yet?' she asked James.

'No.' He groaned with frustration and re-focused his binoculars. 'Hang on. Where are you looking? Oh! I can see it now. It's fantastic! I wonder if it's one of the tagged leopards.'

'Probably,' Mandy said. 'Maybe it's Tommy. That was the other one whose signal we heard in the office. It can't be Leela.' Sandie's special leopard was far away in the north of the reserve, where it was dry and wild and free from the prying eyes of tourists. Maybe she was resting in a tree too, Mandy thought, waiting for night to fall so she could hunt for food for her hungry cubs.

Three

'You were lucky to spot Jomo,' Lindiwe said.

Mandy and James were in the Ngomanes' kitchen at the base, helping Lindiwe and her mother prepare dinner. The kitchen had wooden walls painted sky blue and decorated with woven hangings. The room was empty except for a cooker, a table and chairs.

'I almost didn't see him!' Mandy told her. 'It was his tail that gave him away.'

Lindiwe grinned. 'A leopard's tail is never still.'

Sandie had told them that the leopard they'd seen was an adult male, but not Tommy. 'Jomo's radio signals were picked up in this area a few days ago. We think he might have fathered Leela's cubs,' she had said.

Mmatsatsi Ngomane was slim and elegant and wore a traditional red and black dress. Now she lifted some food out of a saucepan, piled it on to a plate, then covered it with a snowy white cloth.

Lindiwe's eyes gleamed. She lifted a corner of the cloth and sneaked a taste.

Her mother wagged a finger at her. 'Where are your manners, you terrible girl!' she grumbled good-naturedly.

Lindiwe just grinned and gave her mum an affectionate hug. 'Fried *sudza* balls and sweet relish! And *putu*. My favourite!' she told Mandy and James.

'It looks delicious,' Mandy agreed. 'What's it made from?'

'*Sudza* is cooked corn meal,' Mmatsatsi told her. And *putu* is a sort of sweet made from rice, peanuts and sugar.'

Mandy carried a bowl of relish outside to the veranda, where her parents, Sipho and Sandie were seated. The velvet darkness of the African night was all around, but lanterns shed a cheerful light over the tables and benches. She loved the night chorus of birds and insects.

Lindiwe, her mum, and James followed her with the rest of the food and placed it on the table.

'Thanks, Mmatsatsi,' Sandie exclaimed. 'This is a feast.'

Mandy sat down at the table and heaped her plate with the *sudza* balls. She thought of Levina, out in the bush, probably camping in a tent. It seemed a shame that she wasn't here to enjoy the party, but Mandy knew that the scientist was doing the work she loved best.

After the meal, Sipho got up and went inside. 'He's gone to fetch his pride and joy,' Mmatsatsi told them. 'I hope you can play!'

Intrigued, Mandy waited to see what Sipho would bring out. He appeared a few moments later with a small folding pool table and four battered hand-carved cues.

'Brilliant!' James enthused, jumping up to help Sipho set up the table. 'Who's for a game?'

'Why don't you and Mandy play?' Lindiwe suggested.

Once the table was set up, everyone watched as James squinted down the cue, lining up for his break shot. The balls all rolled in different directions and a striped ball dropped into a corner pocket. 'Right. I'm striped and you're plain, Mandy,' he said.

James potted another ball.

'Good shot, James!' Lindiwe encouraged him. James blushed and fluffed his next shot.

'Oh, hard luck.' Mandy picked up a cue and aimed for a well-placed plain ball. It went straight into a pocket. 'Yes!' She managed to pocket three more plain balls before missing the fourth. 'Your turn again, James.'

James had obviously overcome his embarrassment and soon cleared the table of striped balls. The last ball whizzed across the table and dropped into the pocket with a plop.

'Well done!' Mandy said generously. 'Why don't you play James now, Lindiwe?'

Mandy could hear monkeys chittering in the nearby trees as she settled back into her chair to watch. The sharp scent of marigolds floated on the night breeze. What a wonderful holiday this was turning out to be!

'Hi.' Lindiwe raised a hand to greet Mandy and James when they arrived outside the main reception building the next morning. David

McKenzie was with her. 'We thought we'd both show you round.'

'Great.' Mandy was eager to get going. 'Where are we going?'

'The nature trail, maybe?' David suggested. Lindiwe wrinkled her nose.

'I think we should go and see Kubi and Ushukela.'

'Who are they?' Mandy asked.

David grinned mysteriously and glanced at Lindiwe. 'Ushukela's our friend,' he said. 'And Kubi—'

'I think we should start with Kubi,' Lindiwe interrupted.

'No. he'll probably still be asleep!' David said, shaking his head. 'You know how grumpy he is until he's eaten . . .'

Lindiwe and David couldn't seem to agree where to start the tour. Intrigued, Mandy and James exchanged glances as they waited for their new friends to make up their minds.

'Maybe we should start walking?' Mandy suggested.

'OK,' Lindiwe agreed. 'Let's go round to the back of the hotel.'

Mandy and James walked on past a dark green

bush with huge pink flowers. Colourful butterflies flew back and forth, and fine red dust powdered their trainers.

Lindiwe and David were a little way behind, still arguing. Mandy began to wonder if they would ever make a joint decision. She decided to make for one of the rest areas, where tables and chairs were set out around a small pool. A group of guests were just leaving, and a tray with coffee cups and biscuits was left on the table.

Suddenly a monkey leaped agilely over the back of a chair and took a dive beneath the table where a broken biscuit lay on the grass.

'Vervet monkeys!' Mandy had seen the slim light-coloured monkeys with their black feet and black tail tips, before.

With a screech, two more monkeys jumped on to the tabletop and began gathering up crumbs with nimble fingers.

'Wow! Look at them!' James pointed to three hyraxes, which were rushing forward to join in. One of them scuttled up on to the table.

'It's everyone for himself!' Mandy laughed, stopping to watch. One of the monkeys chittered angrily at the hyrax on the tabletop, startling it into dropping a piece of biscuit. Nimbly, the monkey snatched the morsel from under its nose and darted away. The hyrax stood up on its back legs, squealing and grunting angrily.

'It's brave, isn't it? That monkey's twice its size!' Mandy was impressed with the little animal's determination.

By now David and Lindiwe had caught up. 'Dassies have a bad temper for little animals!' Lindiwe told them.

'Dassies?' James sounded puzzled.

'That's what we call hyraxes,' David explained. 'Did you know they're the closest relatives of elephants?'

Mandy stared in astonishment. 'How come?'

'Their front teeth are really tiny tusks,' Lindiwe said. 'And they have three toes – like elephants.'

It seemed amazing, Mandy thought. The tiny creatures couldn't look more different from elephants.

'Sophie's got a hyrax for a pet,' David remarked.

'We know! We've met Dilly.' Mandy told him how the hyrax had jumped into the swimming-pool, and laughed at the memory of her dad's face.

Soon all the biscuit crumbs had been snapped up and the animals melted back into the nearby bushes. 'Oh, bother!' James said, frowning. 'I didn't take any photographs!'

'Never mind,' Mandy consoled him. 'There'll be loads to photograph when we go out with Sandie tomorrow. You should get some amazing photos of Leela and her cubs.'

James nodded. 'That's going to be great. I'm taking lots of film, just in case we see a black panther as well . . .'

Mandy smiled. They both knew how rare black panthers were, but James could be very determined. He had what her grandad called 'staying power'.

'Come on, this way,' Lindiwe called, leading them round the back of the hotel.

The doors of the kitchen were open and a man wearing a huge white apron stood in the doorway. '*Sawubona*, Lindiwe, David!' he greeted them and waved them over. 'Here! Food for your animals.' He handed them a bag stuffed full of vegetable scraps.

'*Ngiyabonga*, Kitunga,' Lindiwe thanked him. 'They'll enjoy this.'

Lindiwe took the bag and led the others towards a cluster of wooden sheds.

Mandy adjusted her baseball cap and followed.

She glanced at James. 'I think we're finally about to meet Ushukela and Kubi,' she whispered.

In front of the sheds there was an area of flat grassy scrub. Mandy saw a large sandy-coloured antelope, standing beneath the shade of a thorn tree. It had long straight horns, with a spiral twist down their length. It lifted its head and looked at them.

'Oh!' Mandy breathed. 'It's beautiful.'

'He's an eland.' David looked pleased. He pursed his lips and gave a soft whistle. 'Ushukela! Ushukela, come and see what we've got for you!'

The eland sniffed the air, smelling the vegetable scraps. Then suddenly he trotted towards them. Mandy and James felt the vibration underfoot as Ushukela's hooves struck the hard-baked ground.

'Wow! He's . . . er . . . big, isn't he?' James eyed the long, sharp horns warily, as the eland got nearer.

'Yes.' David said proudly. 'He's 170 centimetres at the shoulder and weighs almost a tonne.'

Ushukela stopped suddenly, coming to a halt in a cloud of red dust less than a metre away. Mandy's head was nearly level with the eland's shoulder and she saw the solid muscle rippling beneath the sandy coat.

'Don't worry. He's very tame,' David told them reassuringly. 'His name means "sugar" in isiZulu. That's because he's so sweet-tempered.' He laughed, and fished in the bag for a handful of carrot peelings. The eland snorted eagerly, reaching forward to nibble the vegetables.

Mandy reached out slowly and stroked Ushukela's narrow, sandy nose. 'Do you want to feed him?' David asked, offering her some of the food.

Mandy took some of the peelings in her hand, flattening her palm the way she did when she fed horses at home in Yorkshire. Ushukela's mobile lips tickled her fingers as he drew the food into his mouth.

'Do you want a go, James?' David offered.

James nodded and began feeding the eland, when, suddenly, a harsh, angry-sounding shriek rang out.

'Oh!' Mandy almost jumped out of her skin.

She whipped round and saw a large bird stalking towards them from one of the wooden sheds. It was very handsome, with black shiny plumage and a bright red face and beak. Planting its strong feet squarely with each waddling step, it came towards them open-beaked, its large red-rimmed eyes glinting with annoyance.

Lindiwe grinned at their shocked expressions. 'Meet Kubi. He's a ground hornbill. His name means "bad".' She had to yell above the noise, as the bird continued to shriek and demand attention.

Mandy laughed, but James didn't look too keen to get to know the bad-tempered bird better.

The hornbill walked boldly beneath the eland's legs. It looked up and screeched bossily.

Lindiwe bent down and scattered a handful of salad scraps on the grass. 'Here you are, Kubi. Plenty for you.'

The screeching stopped like magic. Kubi made a soft crooning in his throat and curled one horny foot around the food. Holding a piece of red pepper, he pecked at it delicately.

Mandy and James watched the transformation open-mouthed.

'He doesn't like to be left out,' Lindiwe explained. 'And he's only bad-tempered when he's hungry.'

'Which is all the time!' David added.

'No, it's not!' Lindiwe defended her pet.

'Oh no?' David raised his eyebrows questioningly.

'Well anyway, Ushukela doesn't mind him making a noise,' Lindiwe told them, stroking the eland. 'He likes Kubi.'

It was true. The eland was munching away, oblivious to the big bird standing between his front legs. Mandy laughed at the unlikely friendship. At least the eland and the hornbill were less argumentative than their owners!

Mandy and James spent the rest of the day

exploring the resort with Lindiwe and David. At about six o'clock they walked back to the research base. They found Mr and Mrs Hope helping Sandie prepare for their trip.

'Insect repellent, first-aid kit, sunblock . . .' Emily ticked off items on a checklist as Sandie named them.

Mr Hope joined them by the Land-rover. 'Hello. Had an interesting day?' he asked.

Mandy nodded and told them all about David and Lindiwe's pets. Emily laughed when she heard about Kubi's bad temper. 'Hmm. Reminds me of someone else I know, who isn't human until he's had his first cup of tea!'

Mr Hope looked innocent. 'Can't think who you mean.'

'Right. Almost finished here . . .' Sandie closed the lid of a storage box. 'Hello . . . here's Sophie.'

Mandy turned to see that Sophie was hurrying towards them with Dilly clutched in her arms. The younger girl was out of breath and her face was blotchy as if she'd been crying.

Mandy hurried over to meet Sophie, but David got there first. 'What's the matter, Soph?' he asked anxiously.

'Oh, David. Someone's stolen Tasha!' Sophie

blurted out her news, and two large tears rolled down her cheeks as she gulped for breath. 'And . . . and I was so worried that they'd come here too and steal Ushukela and Kubi. So I ran straight over to check up on them . . .'

David looked shocked. 'Are they all right?'

Sophie nodded. 'But poor Tasha's not. She's gone!'

Seeing Mandy and James's questioning faces, David explained. 'Tasha's a tame oribi. She belongs to a friend of Mum and Dad's who runs a small hotel a few kilometres away.'

'Oh no!' Mandy hated to think of anyone losing their pet. She had seen oribi on previous visits to Africa. They were small antelopes, very beautiful with their long slender necks and silky coats of pale reddish-brown.

'How do you know she's been stolen, Sophie?' Emily Hope asked, calm and reasonable as usual. 'Could there have been a mistake?'

Sophie shook her head, sniffing and wiping her eyes. 'I was in the hotel office when Mum took the phone call.' She looked up at her brother. 'Do you think they will come back and steal our pets?'

'I don't think anyone could get near to them,' David reassured her. 'With the research base here, there are too many people around to keep an eye on them.' He looked fierce.

'But why would anyone steal a tame oribi?' James looked puzzled.

'I'm afraid it sounds like smugglers.' Sandie produced a tissue and handed it to Sophie. 'Animals are sometimes smuggled out of the country for unscrupulous private collectors. Tasha's used to being handled by humans. I expect that made it easier to steal her. Fortunately oribi aren't rare, although that's no excuse. But endangered species are always at risk.'

'How could anyone be so cruel?' Mandy felt angry and upset.

Her dad put a hand on her shoulder. 'I know, it's awful,' he said. 'Fortunately smugglers and the like are in the minority. There are far more people, like Sandie and Sipho, who only care about the animals.'

'I know,' Mandy replied. 'It's just that the few troublemakers do so much damage.'

'What your dad says is true,' Lindiwe told Mandy. 'People here care about the land – and most people understand that protecting the wildlife is part of caring for our land and for ourselves.'

Mandy nodded, but she still felt angry, thinking of the stolen oribi and her worried owner. And she couldn't help wondering – were all the other animals in the area safe?

Four

Mandy, James, and Mr and Mrs Hope arrived at the base early the following morning. Sandie's battered Land-rover was fully loaded with boxes of supplies. Her jacket lay across the front seat, but there was no sign of Sandie herself.

They found her and Sipho in the office, sitting in front of the radio. Sandie looked up when they entered and gave a brief, distracted smile.

'Hello, everyone. There's been a bit of a hold-up. We've been having problems getting a clear fix on Leela's whereabouts. I want to do a final check before we set off.'

Mandy and James watched in silence as Sipho

pressed buttons. The radio crackled and fizzed as he searched for the frequency for Leela's signal. More static crackled over the line, then there came a weak bleep, bleep.

'Got her! But the signal's very faint.' Sipho leaned forward, listening intently.

Sandie moved the red pins on the map, checking Leela's new position. 'She's moving further northwards, away from the river. That's outside her usual territory.'

'Oh.' Suddenly, Mandy realised that the faint bleeps had stopped completely. She bit her lip, afraid that something had happened to the leopard.

Sipho pressed buttons, switching frequencies, but it was no use. At last, he turned to Sandie. 'We've lost her. That's strange.'

Mandy frowned. 'Maybe her tag's come loose,' she suggested helpfully. 'Like that young male leopard's the first day we arrived.'

James shook his head. 'But if the tag was lying on the ground, the signal would stay in one place, wouldn't it?'

Sandie nodded.

'Oh, of course.' Mandy felt a bit foolish. James was always so logical.

'We've established that Leela's moving northwards.' Sandie sounded puzzled. 'It looks like she's wandered out of range of our transmitter.'

'But what about her cubs?' Mandy asked.

'Leela could be moving them to safer territory because of some threat. But it's always possible that the cubs are dead or sick,' Sandie answered calmly. 'We think the cubs are about eight weeks old, so they're still entirely dependent on their mother.'

Mandy shuddered at the thought of the cubs lying injured or dead.

'Couldn't Leela just be hunting for food?' James asked.

'It's unlikely in daylight,' Sandie said.

'No,' Mandy agreed. 'Leopards hunt at night, don't they? Maybe she's looking for better cover for her cubs.'

'It's unlikely, Mandy.' Sipho Ngomane shook his head. 'There would be plenty of cover amongst the rocks and trees near the river.'

'Then why would she move from such a favourable place?' Mrs Hope echoed Mandy's own thoughts.

'I'm not sure.' Sandie frowned and ran her

fingers through her short hair. 'It could be a number of things. Another leopard or a pride of lions might have moved into her territory. Something's alarmed her, though.' She turned to Sipho. 'We're all ready to go out and look for her anyway. We can get to her last known position and take a look around.'

Sipho turned off the radio and pushed his chair away from the desk. 'Makes sense,' he agreed. 'She's likely to respond to you.'

Mandy waited quietly. She was eager to get going.

'OK.' Sandie reached up to a shelf for a small portable radio transmitter, then slipped some spare batteries into the pocket of her sleeveless jacket. 'We'll need to keep in touch and there are no phone links that far out in the reserve,' she explained.

Sipho rose to his feet and unlocked a gun case. 'I'm coming too. You may want an experienced tracker and you'll need a guard – just in case you stumble on a sleeping buffalo,' he added, grinning at Mandy and James.

Sandie laughed. 'Ready?' she asked. They all nodded. 'Then let's go.'

Mandy followed the others out to the Land-rover, her mind still teeming with questions. What had disturbed Leela so much that she had wandered so far from her usual territory?

The Land-rover sped over the dry landscape, bumping and jolting down the stony track and stirring up clouds of red dust.

Sipho pointed out various animals as they passed. Mandy hung out of the window to take in the sight of gazelles on either side. A springbok, startled by the rumbling noise of the engine, suddenly took off, leaping about two metres in the air before dropping down and then shooting up high again.

'Look at that! It's "pronking",' James said.

Mandy grinned. The springbok's jumping movement was just the same as that of the fallow deer in Glisterdale Forest back in Yorkshire.

The sun had risen high in the sky by now. Sandie drove steadily. As they progressed northwards, the landscape became flatter, opening out into true savannah. There were fewer trees now, just a seemingly endless stretch of bleached grass and tough, spiky bushes. Here the sun baked the land hard and a heat haze shimmered in the distance.

Mandy settled back in her seat. She stared over

Sandie's shoulder, peering intently towards a line of purple-brown hills.

'Leela's usual territory is just beyond that ridge,' Sandie told them. 'When we get there, we'll stop and see if we can pick up her signal on the radio.'

'How long will it take us to reach the ridge?' James wanted to know.

'Another hour or so, then a bit longer to reach the river,' Sandie replied. 'We'll have a few hours to look for her and then we'll need to find one of the trail camps to spend the night. I'm afraid they're pretty basic. Nothing like Ubungane Lodge!'

'I don't think Mandy and James will mind,' Emily Hope said.

Mandy smiled at her mum.

'Rhinos on our left,' Sandie said, braking gently.

Two rhinos were watching the Land-rover's rumbling approach; their small eyes seemed wary and hostile. They had enormous curved horns and their tough, leathery skin hung in folds. 'Oh, look! Aren't they brilliant?' Mandy breathed. Suddenly, the huge animals took fright and lumbered off across the plain, raising clouds of red dust.

'Phew! I'm glad they didn't decide to charge.'

Mr Hope pretended to be relieved. He wadded his jacket behind his back, cushioning himself from the bumps and jolts of the Land-rover as it crossed the rough terrain. 'I've been meaning to ask you, Sandie. How did you come to rear an orphaned leopard cub?'

Mandy and James leaned forward, keen to hear how Sandie had found Leela.

'Leela was found by a hunting party and handed over to a park ranger,' Sandie told them. 'The ranger brought her to the game warden there, who happened to be a friend of mine. He knew I'd already reared a lion and a cheetah cub, so he contacted me to see if I'd take Leela.'

Mandy hadn't known about the lion and cheetah cubs. 'What happened to those other cubs?' she asked. 'Did you release them into the wild too?'

Sandie nodded. 'They live in a reserve in Kenya now.'

'That's great,' Mandy said, delighted that the fully-grown lion and cheetah could live out their lives in the wild.

'You said a hunting party found Leela?' Adam Hope asked.

'That's right,' Sandie told him. 'They said she

was abandoned. I'm not so sure she wasn't orphaned.'

Mandy went cold all over. 'You mean the hunters killed Leela's mother?'

'Perhaps. We'll never know the truth. They had permits to shoot certain types of game – but not leopards.'

Mandy frowned, feeling angry. She hated hunting.

Her dad, who was sitting next to her, noticed her expression. 'I don't like the idea of hunting either, love. But at least it's strictly regulated these days. And it does bring valuable revenue into the country.'

'Your dad's right.' Sipho Ngomane nodded agreement. 'That money helps with the conservation of many other animals and the environment. And in turn, that benefits the communities of people who have to live here too.'

Mandy had heard this argument before. She knew it made sense, but in her heart she would never come to terms with the idea of healthy animals being killed for sport.

Mandy's mum squeezed her shoulder. 'At least Leela survived. How old was she when she came to you, Sandie?' she asked.

'Well – the ranger who'd been looking after her thought she must be about two months old. But I think she was nearer three months.'

'How did you know?' Mandy hung on to the side of the Land-rover, swaying with the movements of the vehicle as they crossed a dried-up river bed.

'Well, I've seen plenty of cubs! Leela was large for her age and her markings were particularly striking. Forest leopards are always bigger and much darker than low-country leopards. Leela has ten parallel rosettes on her spine. Many leopards have maybe two or three pairs that match up like that. Some have no regular markings.'

'Oh,' Mandy breathed. 'She sounds beautiful. I can't wait to meet her.'

James had leaned forward to listen. 'Shouldn't Leela really be living in a forest?' he asked, practical as ever.

Sandie nodded. 'Ideally, yes. But we couldn't find a suitable reserve with a large enough territory. We needed somewhere where she wouldn't be threatened by lions or other leopards. I was very concerned that she'd find it difficult to adapt to the arid country here, but she settled into the *boma* we built for her without any trouble at all.'

'And you had to become her mother!' Mandy said, her eyes shining, as she thought of Sandie taking care of the tiny, helpless cub.

'That's right. It was fortunate that Leela was young enough for me to be imprinted on her.'

'That's why you were able to develop such a strong bond?' said Mrs Hope.

'Yes. Leela was always very trusting, affectionate and good-natured with me. She's different now of course – she's fully wild. I have to be careful to remember that.' Sandie fell silent and stared out of the windscreen, looking towards the distant ridge.

About half an hour later, they stopped in the shade of some rocks to eat a packed lunch. Mandy was glad of the break. She felt hot and was aching from being jolted about on the stony tracks. Emily Hope reached into a cool box and handed round egg and tomato sandwiches and cold drinks.

'Thanks, Mum,' Mandy said, biting into her sandwich. 'These are great.'

After a short rest, they all got back into the Land-rover and pressed on. Sipho took a turn driving and it was past midday when they crossed a wide sweep of grassland and began ascending the ridge.

Sandie asked Sipho to stop the car and switched on the radio transmitter. 'If Leela has doubled back towards the river, she'll come into range again and we'll pick up her signal,' she said hopefully.

Mandy listened to the now familiar crackle of static as Sandie tried to get a fix on Leela's frequency. After a while, Sandie shook her head. 'No luck yet. Let's go a bit further on.'

Sipho steered carefully round a boulder and Mandy caught sight of a river up ahead. A single, black-faced baboon peered curiously down at them from a rocky ledge as they passed. It yawned, showing a gaping red mouth and huge teeth.

'I'll slow down now,' Sipho said, a few minutes later, 'so you can get a better look, Sandie.' The engine roar fell to a murmur as the Land-rover crept towards the lush growth along the banks. Here, ironwood and ebony trees grew tall and strong.

As Sipho slowed to a halt, Sandie opened the car door. 'I'm going to get out and call to her. She might come to me if she's in the area.'

'Shall we help her look?' Mandy asked, glancing across at James who nodded and reached for his door.

'No. You stay in the Land-rover,' Sipho said firmly. 'It could be dangerous. I'm going to drive along slowly and keep up with her.'

'Sipho's right,' Mrs Hope agreed. 'Besides, Leela might not respond to Sandie's calls if strangers are moving around.'

'OK,' Mandy sighed. She knew they were right, but she never found it easy to sit and wait.

Mandy watched as Sandie scrambled over large

rocks and boulders calling, 'Leela! Leela!'

Mandy peered through her binoculars, scanning the area around the river. She caught sight of a single file of wildebeest in the distance, their strange thick necks and large heads drooping in the heat. A herd of slim brown impala were drinking downstream, but there was no sign of a leopard. 'Can you see anything, James?' she asked.

James shook his head.

By now, Sandie had climbed the ridge and Mandy watched her pacing up and down across the skyline, calling for Leela. Sipho kept pace with her in the Land-rover as she searched the caves and crevices along the river. Mandy and James watched through their binoculars, scanning the plain for a glimpse of a leopard.

Eventually Sandie returned to the Land-rover, looking hot and dusty. 'Nothing,' she said, unable to hide her disappointment. 'I've looked everywhere. There's no sign of Leela or her cubs.' She climbed into the car and accepted the can of lemonade that Emily offered her from the cool box. 'Thanks, Emily.'

Mandy had raised her binoculars and trained them on a patch of reeds down-river. She focused on the herd of gazelle at the water's edge. One of them looked up. It froze for a second, then skittered backwards in alarm.

'Oh.' She tensed and gripped James's arm. 'Over there!'

'What is it?' he asked, frowning.

'Something's spooking that gazelle,' Mandy said.

Her parents and Sipho all turned to look. 'She's right!' Sipho said, lowering his binoculars and edging the Land-rover forward a few more metres.

Mandy was still studying the startled gazelle which was definitely reacting to something hiding in the long reeds. The other gazelles clustered together, milling about, apparently undecided whether to make a run for it.

By now, they were all staring intently out of the windows.

'It could be Leela, stalking them,' Mandy murmured.

'Sandie couldn't pick up her signal, remember?' her dad reminded her. 'Let's wait and see.'

The gazelles were standing in the shallows, still shifting nervously. Mandy saw their flared nostrils, their ears twitching with alarm. Suddenly, one broke free from the herd. Others turned to follow. Then the whole herd fled along the river.

Oh, please let it be Leela! Mandy thought. All her senses alert, she kept watch for any sign of the predator. Suddenly, her keen eyes picked out the animal moving stealthily through the reeds. She saw a slim, spotted shape and watched as it leaned forward, muscles bunched, ready to break cover. Mandy's heart missed a beat. 'Look!' she hissed, clutching at James's arm. 'I think it's Leela . . .'

Five

A moment later, a cheetah leaped out of the reeds, its slender powerful body flexing as it sped across the shallows.

'Oh.' Mandy's hopes crashed and she let out a low sigh of disappointment. As the cheetah pounced on one of the gazelles, she lowered her binoculars. She didn't feel brave enough to watch the predator make its kill.

Mr Hope turned and gave her a sympathetic smile. 'We'll find Leela yet. Think how lucky we are to have seen a cheetah!'

'I know. It was great. I just wish it was a leopard . . .' She wrinkled her nose at her dad.

'You know what I mean.'

He nodded. 'I know. Never mind, love.'

After the false alarm, everyone seemed subdued. Emily Hope handed round more cool drinks. Mandy passed one to James and drank hers gratefully.

'Maybe Leela's just found a new den in a new territory further away and taken the cubs to it,' she suggested.

'I hope so,' James said with feeling.

Sandie flashed them a tired grin. 'I was just thinking the same thing. The fact that there are baboons here now would explain why she might have moved on. Maybe I've been worrying too much.' She had been spreading out her map. For a few moments she studied the area where Leela's last signals had petered out. Then Mandy saw her face brighten as she tapped the map with her finger. 'I think she could have been heading here. Look, these three outcrops form a valley.'

Sipho bent close to investigate. 'It's the only other place between here and the northern edge of the reserve where there's enough cover to make a lair. But we're not going to be able to get there until tomorrow evening. And there's no guarantee that Leela and her cubs will be there.'

Sandie wiped her dusty face with her hand and sighed. 'I know it's a long shot, but I've got a really strong hunch. I think we should check it out.'

'Me too!' Mandy felt better already. 'Maybe Leela and her cubs have just found a better place to hide. Can't we go and look now?' she asked eagerly.

'It'll be dark in a couple of hours, love,' Mr Hope pointed out. 'We can't drive through the night, remember. It's too dangerous.'

'Your dad's right,' Sipho said. 'This is wild country. We can't take risks out here.'

Mandy nodded. She knew that dusk fell quickly in the African bush, and once it was dark, Sipho and Sandie wouldn't be able to see well enough to drive safely. But there had to be a solution.

'It would be good to get a bit further tonight . . .' Sandie said thoughtfully, studying the map. 'If we press on past the rest camp it would cut hours off tomorrow's journey.'

'But where would we stay?' Emily Hope sounded concerned.

'Here, at Letaba House.' Sandie showed her the map and pointed to another camp farther to the north. 'It's a small hotel. The people who run it are friends of mine. We can just reach it by nightfall if we start out now.'

'OK, everyone. Let's go!' Sipho climbed into the driver's seat and started the engine.

The sun was sinking below the horizon as the Land-rover approached the gate with its carved wooden sign saying 'Letaba House'.

Mandy felt hot and tired and desperately in need of a shower.

'Hey! Watch out!' Sipho had to swerve to avoid a speeding jeep as he pulled into the carpark.

Mandy got a quick glimpse of the other vehicle. It was painted a glossy black and had heavy silver crash-bars. She couldn't see the driver through the tinted windows.

'More late-comers,' Mr Hope said.

'And in a hurry too!' James stared after the modern jeep.

Sipho parked the Land-rover in the carpark and Sandie went into the reception. She emerged a few minutes later, beckoning them to follow her. 'Our huts are just over here.'

Mandy followed her to the grass-roofed huts, grouped beside a stream and shaded by kuduberry trees. 'Isn't this great!' she exclaimed.

She and James were sharing a hut. Inside there

was just enough room for two beds. The low grass roof rose into a cone shape above their heads. 'I bet it's full of spiders,' James said. 'Your dad will love that.'

Mandy laughed. If there was one creature her dad couldn't stand, it was spiders.

It was beginning to feel cooler now and Mandy went to fetch her fleece jacket from the Land-rover in the carpark. It always amazed her that the African night could be so cold after the fierce heat of the day. James walked with her.

'Look! That posh jeep's parked just over there,' Mandy observed.

'It's pretty impressive, isn't it?' James said, walking over to examine the jeep. 'Look at that mascot. And the back is completely closed in. I bet it's got air-conditioning too.'

Mandy frowned, looking at the silver eagle mascot on the bonnet. She thought the black jeep was too flashy. 'I think I prefer Sandie's Land-rover,' she said. 'It might be scruffy, but it's better for watching animals. At least it's camouflaged.'

'Hey! What are you two doing snooping around?' an angry voice called out.

Mandy whipped round. A muscular man wearing a fawn safari suit and heavy boots was

striding towards them. He stopped and looked down at them, feet planted apart and hands on his hips.

'Well?' he said. 'Speak up!'

'We're not doing anything,' James said nervously.

'We were only looking at your jeep,' Mandy added.

The man scowled. He had fair hair and his face was red with sunburn. His small hard eyes scanned their faces. At last he seemed to be satisfied. 'OK, then. But if I was you, I wouldn't hang around here,' he warned them.

Just then, two other men appeared from one of the huts. 'Got a problem, Ben?' one of them called.

'Nah. It's just nosy kids,' came the dismissive reply. With a final glance at Mandy and James, he walked over to meet his friends.

Mandy was angry, but she clenched her jaw to stop herself from answering back. There was something about the man that made her uneasy. 'Come on, James,' she said.

Adam and Emily Hope were standing outside when Mandy and James got back. 'What was all that about?' Mandy's dad asked.

She explained how the man had objected to them looking at the jeep.

'People can be very possessive about their cars,' Emily Hope commented. 'I wouldn't take it personally, if I were you. Come on. Let's freshen up, then go and eat.'

After a quick visit to one of the wooden wash-huts, Mandy felt much better. She was looking forward to the meal. Sandie and Sipho were waiting outside their hut with Mr and Mrs Hope, when Mandy and James emerged. Sipho had changed into clean khaki shorts and a shirt with the research base logo on the breast pocket.

They walked up to the main building where there was a small restaurant on the veranda. As Mandy entered the dining area and took a seat, she saw that the three men from the jeep were sitting at the end table. They glanced across, warily.

Adam Hope smiled at them. 'Good evening,' he said pleasantly. There was no reply. The three men looked away and went back to talking amongst themselves.

'Charming!' James said, sitting down next to Sipho.

'Not very friendly, are they?' Sandie remarked in a low voice.

'No! They're not!' Mandy told her how the large fair-haired man had warned them to stay away from the jeep.

Sandie's expression changed. She glanced across at the men. 'They seem to be taking a great interest in Sipho now. I wonder why?'

Mandy realised that Sandie was right. One of the men kept giving Sipho Ngomane nervous glances and then whispering something to his companions.

The waitress came and took their orders. When

Adam Hope had chosen from the menu, he turned to Mandy and James. 'Why don't you ask Sandie about black panthers, you two?' he suggested. 'You are still interested in them, aren't you?'

Mandy grinned at her dad. 'Of course we are!' She smiled at Sandie. 'James showed me your article,' she began.

'Er . . . yes.' James blushed as he turned towards Sandie. 'Um . . . Sandie? You know that article you wrote about big cats, for *Animal Planet* magazine?'

'Yes, I remember.' Sandie nodded. 'Did you enjoy it?'

'It was brilliant,' James said enthusiastically. 'All that stuff about lions and tigers and pumas was great – only there wasn't very much about black panthers . . .'

'Oh dear. Sorry about that!' Sandie's lips twitched in a good-natured smile. 'Fire away then. What do you want to know about them?'

'Is it true that black panthers are really just leopards?' James asked.

'That's right,' Sandie confirmed. 'Occasionally a black cub will be born to normal spotted parents. It's due to a recessive gene – the same kind of gene that can produce a blue-eyed child from two brown-eyed parents.'

'So can black panthers and leopards inter-breed?' Mandy wanted to know.

'Yes, they can,' Sandie replied. 'That's how we first knew that they're definitely the same species. Black panthers are just melanistic leopards.'

'Melanistic?' Mandy asked, puzzled.

'It means they have more than the normal amount of melanin – that's the dark pigment that makes your skin tan in the sun,' Mr Hope explained.

'If you ever got near enough, you would see the normal rosette markings in the dark coat,' Sandie told them.

'Wow! Could you see that much detail through binoculars?' James asked.

Sandie smiled. 'Possibly, but I don't think you'll get the chance to do that in a hurry. No one's seen a black panther in this reserve for a few years.'

Mandy nudged James in the ribs.

'Never mind,' said Emily Hope. 'I think we'd all be more than happy just to see Leela and her cubs!'

'I'll second that,' Mr Hope agreed.

Mandy looked around the veranda. She realised

that the waitress was clearing the half-eaten remains of a meal away from the empty end table. 'That's funny,' she said to James. 'Those men have gone. But I'm sure they didn't come past us. I thought this was the only entrance into the dining room.'

'It is,' James observed. 'They must have hopped over the railings.'

Mandy noticed that Sandie too was looking thoughtfully towards the empty table.

After everyone had finished eating, they wandered back through reception. The hotel proprietor looked up from the desk and smiled. 'Did you enjoy your meal?' she asked.

'It was delicious, thanks,' Sandie said.

'Yes,' Mrs Hope said. 'Thanks very much.'

Sandie hung back from the others to speak to her friend. 'I'll catch you up in a minute,' she called.

'OK,' Mandy said. She and James followed her mum and dad and Sipho back to their huts.

Mandy could hear the sounds of the bush all around, faint howls from far out on the plains, intriguing rustles and squeaks nearby.

'This is great, isn't it?' James said.

Mandy nodded, looking up at the stars, which

seemed close enough to touch. 'I'd be enjoying it even more if we'd found Leela,' she told him. 'I keep thinking about her, wondering where she is and whether her cubs are OK.'

'Me too,' James admitted. 'I just hope they're not hurt.'

'I know.' It was something Mandy could hardly bear to think about.

Back at the huts, they all sat outside on wooden benches, enjoying the coolness of the night. A few minutes later, Sandie joined them and sat down beside Mandy and James.

'Apparently those three men in the jeep are here to look at rare birds. I was curious about them, so I made a few inquiries,' she explained. 'My friend told me they've been staying here for the past couple of nights.'

'Birdwatchers?' Adam Hope looked surprised.

Sandie grinned. 'I know. Appearances can be deceptive, can't they! But this area is known for its rare birds. The wild fruit trees around here are teeming with them.'

James was frowning. He looked across at Mandy. 'I still don't trust those men,' he said in a low voice. 'There's something about them that doesn't seem right.'

'I know what you mean,' Mandy whispered back.

Sandie stretched and rose to her feet. 'Oh, well. I suppose we'd better turn in. We'll need to leave at first light.' She looked down at Mandy and James. 'How are you two at getting up before daybreak?'

James pulled a face.

Mrs Hope answered for them. 'Brilliant when there's an animal rescue involved,' she told Sandie, 'but not so good during term-time!'

Mandy had no problem getting up next morning. She checked her watch and got out of bed. She had hardly slept for worrying about the missing leopard and her cubs. When she did manage to snatch a couple of hours' sleep, she had dreamed of a leopard cub stranded on a tiny rock in the middle of a gushing river.

As she was dressing, James stirred. Groaning, he climbed out of bed and dragged on his clothes. The two of them emerged shivering from the hut to find that the African dawn was only just lighting up the sky.

Sandie was already up and waiting outside. She was holding a water carrier in one hand and a parcel wrapped in greaseproof paper in the other.

'Hi, you two. Couldn't you sleep either? I've been up for half an hour. I thought I may as well make a start on loading up the Land-rover.'

'We'll help you, won't we, James?' Mandy said.

James was polishing his glasses on the bottom of his T-shirt. 'Do you want this box of food putting in the back?' he asked.

'Oh, thanks. I'll put this meat in there.' Sandie said. 'We might need it if we find the cubs.'

'Uh oh. Look over there.' Mandy saw the three men they had met the previous night come out of one of the huts and hurry towards the carpark. Heads down, the men leaped into their jeep and slammed the doors. Moments later, the engine roared into life and the jeep sped off in a cloud of dust.

'Where's the fire?' James asked, as he watched them go.

Sandie turned round just as the jeep screeched around a bend in the road, then disappeared through the main gateway. 'No prizes for guessing who that was!' She stared at the cloud of dust they'd left behind, her brow furrowed in thought. 'I wonder what they were *really* doing here,' she murmured.

Mandy was wondering the same thing. 'I'm sure

that jeep wasn't covered in mud like that last night,' she said.

Something else about the night before was niggling at the back of her mind. It was something about the way the men had hurried away when they had barely finished their meal. If only she could put her finger on it . . .

Six

Ten minutes later, Mandy climbed into the Land-rover and the search for Leela was on again. Despite her worries about the leopard and her cubs, the beauty of the African morning lifted Mandy's spirits. Mist shrouded the plains, softening the harsh outlines of mopane and leadwood trees, and the air was full of birdsong.

'I'll see if I can pick up a signal,' Sandie said, as Sipho pulled up at the side of the track. She turned on the portable radio and began tuning in to Leela's frequency.

Mandy listened hopefully as the radio crackled and fizzed, but there was no bleep from Leela's transmitter tag. She sat staring out of the window as they set off again, silent and thoughtful.

As the sun rose higher, the sky turned an apricot colour. 'Look over there! Giraffe!' James pointed to the horizon.

Mandy could see a tall shape loping towards a cluster of flat-topped thorn trees. It rocked forward on long legs, its neck swaying and dipping as it ran. Then she noticed that a calf was running by its side, keeping perfectly in step with its mother. '*Oh.*' The sight took her breath away.

'Do you two want to stop and have a look?' Sandie turned round in her seat to ask.

Mandy looked across at James and could see that he was as anxious as she was to find Leela. She shook her head. 'Let's go on.'

As they rattled across the plain, they saw no sign of Leela, but instead Mandy caught sight of different kinds of antelope grazing on the tough bleached grass. Sandie and Sipho named them for her; the greyish kudu with its white striped coat and twisted horns, and the fawn-coloured hartebeest.

'Oh, I recognise those!' James pointed to a herd of about thirty eland, large muscular animals with folds of skin called dewlaps hanging from their throats.

'So you should!' Mandy laughed. They were just like David McKenzie's pet, Ushukela.

By midday, everything was still and silent as the reserve baked in the heat. Sandie suggested they stop and rest in the shade. After a lunch of cheese sandwiches and lemonade, brought with them from Letaba House, they set off again.

'The valley's just past those rocks.' Sandie pointed ahead, to where a mass of grey boulders stuck up out of the red earth. 'I just hope Leela's somewhere around here.'

She picked up the radio again and pressed some buttons. Mandy waited for the inevitable crackling of static, but instead she heard the clear bleep, bleep of a radio transmitter tag's signal.

'It's Leela!' Sandie sounded relieved. 'It really is her! Oh, thank goodness!'

'Yes!' Mandy grinned. She couldn't wait to meet the beautiful leopard and her cubs.

'That's brilliant!' James said. 'So all we have to do now is follow the signals.'

The rocky outcrop loomed above them as Sipho drew the Land-rover to a halt beneath some shady acacias.

Sandie was listening intently to the radio. 'The signal's not as strong here,' she said. 'These rocks must be interfering with it.'

'Can you tell which direction the signal's coming from?' Emily Hope asked.

'Directly ahead. Yes, it's quieter, but still clear. Which means she's either somewhere in the valley or just beyond it.' Sandie slipped the small radio into her shirt pocket. 'I think we should take a look.'

'OK. I'll come with you,' said Sipho. 'Everyone else stay inside the Land-rover,' he ordered. 'It could be dangerous.'

'Right,' Mr Hope agreed. 'Call out if you need us.'

Mandy sighed, wishing she could go with Sandie and Sipho. But she contented herself with looking out of the side windows. The entrance to the valley was down a long, gentle slope. She watched as Sandie and Sipho picked their way over the boulder-strewn ground.

Sandie called Leela's name, while Sipho stood on a rock a few metres away from her. Suddenly the air was filled with deafening shrieks. A great troop of baboons came hurtling towards Sandie, their mouths wide open in a display of aggression.

Mandy gasped in horror.

One of the males moved ahead of the others. He was huge, long-muzzled and had a grey mane round his neck and shoulders. He rushed towards Sandie and Sipho on all fours, lips curled back from his huge, fang-like teeth.

Sandie and Sipho stood quite still.

'Oh, no! He's going to attack!' Mandy cried. Then she let out her breath in a sigh of relief as the leading male came to a sudden stop.

'It's probably just a show to frighten them,' Mr Hope reassured her. 'As long as Sipho and Sandie don't make any sudden movements they should be all right.'

Mandy hoped her dad was right. She guessed that there were about fifty baboons. The females were waiting further back, clutching young ones to their chests, while the males sounded their warnings.

Sandie was backing away, feeling her way slowly without turning around. Sipho was doing the same. The leading baboon didn't move any nearer, but he kept up his piercing, challenging barks.

Sipho and Sandie were almost halfway back to the acacias now. Mandy was just starting to relax, when, Sandie's foot suddenly slipped on a smooth rock. She let out a cry and fell down heavily. Mandy saw something drop out of her shirt pocket and slip down the side of a boulder.

'The radio!' Mandy said to James.

The baboons began to back off. Sipho helped Sandie to get up. She winced as she got to her feet. Leaning on Sipho, she hobbled back to the Landrover. Mandy watched the last two baboons as they retreated over the hill.

'It looks as if she's hurt her ankle,' Adam Hope said. He opened the door, ready to help.

'I'll get the first-aid box,' said Emily Hope efficiently.

'They don't realise she's dropped the radio!' Mandy hissed to James.

James craned his neck. 'It's slipped between those two rocks. I can just see it.'

Mandy's keen eyes spotted the small black shape. 'We need that radio. We can't track Leela without it!' She couldn't bear the thought that they might lose Leela and her cubs again now. There was only one thing for it . . .

She glanced across at her parents, who were busy examining Sandie's injury. 'I'll go. Keep quiet, James.'

'Mandy don't . . .' James warned in a whisper. 'It's too dangerous.'

But Mandy ignored her friend's warning. She was already walking towards the rocks, trying not to think about the baboons, but the warning screams had been so loud she couldn't stop herself from trembling. *Just stay where you are now*, she pleaded silently. *I don't want to hurt you or your babies*. She crept slowly up the hill.

Then, nimbly, she scrambled up the rock and reached down into the narrow crack. Her fingers closed over the radio. She gave it a tug, but it didn't move. The radio was jammed! Mandy tried again, inching her fingers forward.

Suddenly a large male rushed forward again. It was barely a metre away, looking down at her from a craggy rock directly above her. Her heart in her mouth, Mandy froze. She knew she mustn't look the animal in the eye or it might think she was challenging it.

The baboon gave another screeching bark. It perched above her, motionless, for what seemed like endless seconds. Then it scurried away on all fours back to the troop.

Mandy breathed a sigh of relief. Turning back to the radio, she quietly worked it free, then began

to move slowly backwards. She was still shaking when she reached the shade where the others stood watching.

'Mandy Hope . . .' Her mother was white-faced with anger.

'I know, Mum. But someone had to get it.' She held up the radio to explain. 'We couldn't find Leela without this. It's lucky I went. It was jammed in that crack and your hands wouldn't have been able to reach it . . .'

'Safety's more important. You nearly gave your dad a heart attack!' Mrs Hope told her furiously.

'But at least you're OK,' her dad said. He gave Mandy a relieved hug. 'But mum's right. Next time, ask us first. I've got enough grey hairs!'

'OK. Sorry,' Mandy said. She handed the radio to Sipho, who began checking it for damage.

'Thank you,' he said calmly. 'It was a foolish thing to do, but very brave. Next time, please ask one of us before dashing off like that.'

Mandy blushed. 'I will,' she promised quietly.

'We really thought that big male was going to attack you,' James whispered.

'So did I!' Mandy said softly. She turned back to her father. 'How's Sandie's leg?' she asked.

Mr Hope had finished his examination. 'Her

ankle's sprained, nothing too serious.' Emily handed him a tube of anti-inflammatory gel and a roll of bandage.

Sandie looked up at them ruefully. 'I knew it would be useful having you two along, but I didn't think it would end up being *me* who needed treatment!'

After the excitement with the baboons, Mandy was glad to relax in the Land-rover while Sipho drove round an overhanging cliff and headed towards open country.

Luckily the radio hadn't been damaged in the fall and Sandie soon picked up the signal again.

'Well – it's pretty clear that we won't find Leela in this valley,' Sandie announced.

Sipho nodded. 'Maybe she moved on because of the baboons?'

'I think you're right,' Sandie agreed. 'She wouldn't risk endangering her cubs.' She paused for a moment to listen to the signals, which were now clear and strong. 'She can't be far away, though.'

'No.' Sipho turned in his seat to speak to the others. 'The edge of the reserve is only just past those trees.' He pointed towards the horizon.

Mandy saw a line of thorns growing along a narrow ridge. She could feel her excitement building. Very soon they would see Leela and her cubs! They drove for another fifteen minutes, Sandie giving Sipho directions as she listened to Leela's signals. Mandy began to feel worried, hoping they would find Leela safe and well.

Suddenly, Sandie called out. 'There! I can see her! She's over by the perimeter fence. Slow down, Sipho!'

Mandy craned her neck to see. The dry yellow grass was long and thick and for a moment she couldn't get a clear view. Then the Land-rover crawled up an incline and she had her first glimpse of Leela.

The leopard was pacing back and forth along a stretch of high chain link fence. Mandy could hear her calling, making rasping, coughing sounds. Then she stopped and reached up at the fence, clawing and chewing at the wire mesh.

'Something's wrong . . .' Mandy murmured.

'Mandy's right,' Sandie said. 'She should be resting during the day.'

Sipho stopped the car. Now they could hear Leela's strange gruff calls more clearly. 'What's the matter with her? Is she sick?' James asked.

'No. She's calling for her cubs,' Sandie said. 'But I can't see them. They ought to be almost at her heels. I'm going over to see what's going on.' She asked Mrs Hope to pass her the cool box, then took out a tightly wrapped package of meat. 'Sipho, wait by the Land-rover, would you? Everyone else stay inside, until I tell you it's safe to get out.'

Sipho nodded and got out of the Land-rover with Sandie.

'This time we *all* stay put.' Adam Hope looked sternly at Mandy.

'OK,' she agreed, too engrossed by her first really close sighting of a wild leopard to protest. It was wonderful to get so close to the powerful animal. She could see the thick coat, richly marked with dark brown rosettes, the large blunt head and the strong limbs that ended in huge paws.

She listened in dismay as Leela continued to call for her cubs, padding back and forth in distress.

By now Sandie was moving closer towards Leela, calling her softly by name. 'Leela. Come, Leela.'

The leopard turned her fierce golden eyes to

look at the approaching woman, her long tail swishing back and forth. Her roundish, wide-set ears flattened and she drew her black lips back from her teeth, growling deep in her throat.

Mandy watched, tense with anticipation. Would Leela recognise her old friend? She knew that animals were at their most dangerous when they had young to protect. The local saying came back to her. 'A leopard is a leopard.' She remembered Sandie telling them that the leopard is the most unpredictable of the big cats.

Leela lifted her blunt nose to sniff the air while her mobile tail lashed at the grass. Then, all at once, she seemed to relax. She gave a rumbling purr and loped slowly towards Sandie.

'Oh!' Mandy was spellbound by the leopard. Fluid muscles moved beneath the glossy spotted coat and the huge paws threw up little clouds of red dust as they dug into the dry ground.

Leela slowed down, walking the last few metres. At the last moment, just when Mandy thought the leopard would collide with Sandie and knock her flying, Leela dropped to the ground. Stretching out to her full length in the grass, she grasped Sandie's lower leg in her front paws and rubbed her head against the woman's foot.

Mandy let out her breath on a long sigh of relief. She slowly relaxed her hunched shoulders and smiled as Leela got to her feet again and licked Sandie's hand.

Sandie chuckled. 'Yes, I'm glad to see you too!' She rubbed her fingers through the thick fur of the leopard's neck, while Leela purred and rubbed against Sandie's hip.

It was just like the behaviour of pet cats at home. 'She's scent marking her!' Mandy exclaimed.

'That's right,' Mr Hope confirmed. 'Just like a domestic cat. It's a way of accepting Sandie as one of her own kind. Quite a privilege for a solitary animal to do that.'

Leela dropped down again, and stretched out on the grass. Sandie spoke softly to her and reached into her pocket for the wrapped package. She drew out a piece of meat and offered it to the leopard. Leela took it gently between her teeth and laid it on the grass, licking it.

While the leopard was occupied, Sandie turned towards the Land-rover where Sipho was waiting with his rifle. She gestured for him to approach. Sipho nodded and walked forward slowly. By now, Leela had bolted the meat down. She looked at Sipho, her golden eyes watchful and alert. She lay on her side at Sandie's feet and allowed Sipho to come right up to her.

'I wonder if we'll get that close to Leela,' James said longingly.

'I suppose it depends on whether Sandie thinks it's safe,' Mrs Hope replied.

Mandy leaned forward eagerly as Sandie and Sipho began walking back towards the Land-rover. Leela was following them! Sandie stopped right beside the Land-rover and gave Leela another piece of meat. The leopard settled down again and began to eat. Sandie motioned for Adam to open the window. 'You can all get out now. Leela will be fine as long as I'm near. I'd like you and Emily to have a look at her. I'm concerned about her. She's just not herself. She seems a bit lethargic, and from the way she's acting, the cubs ought to be near. But there's no sign of them.'

'What do you think has happened to them?' Mandy asked anxiously.

Sandie shrugged her shoulders. 'I don't know. They may be injured, or even dead.'

'Dead?' Mandy felt her heart plummet. Were they really too late?

Seven

With a heavy heart, Mandy climbed out of the Land-rover, followed by James. They watched as Mr Hope bent down to look at the leopard.

'What do you think is wrong, Sandie?' Adam Hope asked.

Sandie paused before replying. 'I don't know. It's just a feeling I've got. Leela's obviously upset and yet, somehow, she seems very subdued. Does that make any sense?'

Adam Hope nodded. 'It's often the first indication that something's wrong. Do you think she'll let me touch her?'

'She should be fine while I'm with her. I'll tell

you when she's fully relaxed.'

Sandie stroked Leela under her chin and spoke to her in a low calming voice. She waited until the leopard's golden eyes narrowed into slits of contentment and a deep purr rumbled in her chest. Leela began licking her paws and rolled on her back, exposing her pale belly to the sun.

'OK. You can go ahead, Adam,' Sandie told him.

Sipho Ngomane stood nearby, leaning against the Land-rover with his rifle propped next to him. He saw Mandy looking at the gun. 'Don't worry,' he told her. 'Only in a life or death situation would I use this.'

'You two stay well back with me, please,' Mrs Hope ordered Mandy and James. 'We don't want to crowd Leela. Too many people around her might unnerve her.'

'OK, Mum,' Mandy said, stepping back. When her mum spoke in that tone, Mandy knew she meant business. Besides, she knew better than to do anything that might upset the leopard and endanger her dad.

They all watched as Mr Hope ran expert hands over Leela. The leopard stared into his face, her mouth open, showing her yellowish bottom teeth as she panted. Now and then she gave a soft growl, but she didn't move.

'What's Dad looking for?' Mandy asked her mum softly.

'I don't expect he knows that himself at this stage,' Emily answered. 'He'll do a routine check, starting with her pulse, then examine her ears, eyes, and nose for signs of infection.'

'A process of elimination?' Mandy smiled up at her mum.

Mrs Hope nodded. 'That's it. We'll make a vet of you yet, Mandy Hope!'

James grinned. 'She's got the best teachers!'

'Hmm, pulse is steady,' Adam Hope reported. 'Her breathing's fine, if anything a little slow, but it's within the normal range. I don't think I'll risk taking her temperature, that might be too much of an intrusion. Ears and nose are fine,' he continued. Stroking Leela's head gently, he looked at her eyes. 'Her pupils are unusually dilated . . .'

Mrs Hope glanced at Mandy. 'The breathing and dilated pupils are probably signs of stress,' she explained. 'Which isn't surprising in the circumstances.'

'No, it's not,' Mandy agreed. 'Poor Leela's been calling and calling for her missing cubs, and there's no sign of them. No wonder she's upset.'

'Have you found anything else?' Sandie was asking Adam.

'Nothing conclusive.' Mr Hope finished his examination and stood up. He gave her his expert opinion. 'Without doing a more detailed check, I'd say Leela's in excellent health. To examine her any more thoroughly, I'd have to sedate her.'

'I don't think that's necessary.' Sandie smiled, looking relieved. 'Maybe my famous intuition's working overtime on this occasion! Thanks for checking her over.'

'No problem.' Mr Hope replied. 'But I expect you've already noticed that she's still producing milk? I'd say she's suckled her cubs fairly recently.'

Sandie stroked Leela's ears as the leopard gave another rumbling purr. 'Yes. I'd noticed that. I'd estimate she last fed them within five or six hours.'

'How long can the cubs survive without their mother's milk?' Mandy asked, worried.

'Probably for a day or two,' Sandie told her. 'Leela will have been giving them small amounts of meat, so they'll have some reserves of body fat.'

Sipho had been listening in silence up to now. He too seemed reassured by Mr Hope's findings.

'The cubs can't have been missing for very long,' he said. 'We should look around to see if we can find any signs of them.'

Mandy looked at Sandie, standing with her hand resting lightly on Leela's head. All that was needed to complete the picture was two lively cubs, still with their baby fluff. Mandy felt a lump in her throat as she remembered the photograph of Leela herself as a baby, on the wall of Leela's Lodge, back at Ubungane Lodge.

Sandie took a deep breath and seemed to be calming herself. 'OK, everyone. I think Sipho's right. I'd like to make sure the cubs aren't lying injured somewhere. Will you all help me look?'

Mandy exchanged a surprised glance with James, then nodded eagerly. If Sandie wasn't ready to believe that the cubs were dead, then neither was she.

Mandy tramped across the tough, spiky grass. It was hot, even for Africa, and the heat haze shimmered on the horizon. She and James had been searching for the missing cubs for about fifteen minutes and already her shirt was damp with sweat.

Sipho Ngomane and her parents were searching

in the scrub by bushes a few metres away.

'Oh!' Mandy almost jumped out of her skin as two huge birds flew up from a nearby ebony tree, startling her. The dark shapes swooped overhead.

'It's OK, they're eagles,' James said.

Mandy gave a shaky laugh. She hadn't realised her nerves were so fragile. 'For a minute there I thought they were vultures!' she confessed.

'I know!' he replied grimly, and Mandy realised he had been thinking the same thought. If the cubs were injured, the vultures would find them before they did.

After another hour of searching the area around the perimeter fence, none of them had found any sign of the cubs.

Everyone stopped for a drink in the shade of the Land-rover, and Mandy took the chance to ask her dad the question that had been worrying her all day.

'Dad? What are the chances of finding Leela's cubs alive?' She knew she could always rely on him to tell her the truth, even when it was hard to take.

'Slim, I'm afraid.' Mr Hope wiped his forehead with a handkerchief. 'The odds of any cubs surviving their first few months aren't good. Life is harsh for youngsters. Lions, hyenas, cheetahs, and all the rest, have to protect their territories otherwise they can't feed their own young.'

Mandy listened, feeling numb because she knew he was right. He had only confirmed what she had been thinking.

'It's a fact of life that you'll never be able to save every animal, love,' her dad said. 'We've had to get used to it. You will too, if you're going to be a vet.'

'I know,' she murmured. She had dealt with animals dying before, but she knew she would never get used to the hollow empty feeling it left in her stomach. 'Thanks, Dad.'

Sandie and Sipho now widened the area of the search. Sipho was checking a thicket of acacias a few metres away. Mandy was dusty, hot and running out of energy. Beside her, James was crouching down near a huge clump of cacti. He peered beneath the thick leathery leaves.

'Found anything?' Mandy asked.

'Not yet.' James's face was red and perspiring beneath his baseball cap. He pushed his damp fringe back under the cap.

'Me neither.' She looked across to where Sandie

was using a long stick to penetrate some spiky bushes. Leela was padding along a few paces behind her. Every now and then she gave another of her rough, coughing calls.

'Poor Leela. I think she knows we're trying to help her find her cubs,' James said.

'But we're not going to, are we? It's hopeless!' Mandy kicked at a hummock of grass in frustration. 'I bet those baboons we saw back in that valley killed them!'

James blinked at her in surprise and stood up. Mandy looked at him sheepishly, and was about to say sorry for her outburst, when she caught sight of something glinting in the grass at her feet.

'What's that?' She nudged the narrow metal tube with the toe of her boot.

James kicked away another tuft of grass. Now Mandy could see a bright blue tag connected to one end of the tube.

'It's a tranquilliser dart!' she exclaimed.

Mandy had seen her mum use one on Chhota, an injured tiger cub that had needed treatment when they had visited the Shere Khan National Park in India.

'You're right!' James bent down, about to pick the dart up.

'No! Don't touch it, James!' she warned. 'It's been fired and that point's sharp!'

James drew back and peered down at the dart. 'But what's it doing here?'

Mandy frowned. 'I think someone may have tried to drug Leela!'

'What?' James's jaw dropped open.

But Mandy was already hurrying towards the tangle of acacias. 'I'll go and fetch mum and dad,' she called over her shoulder. 'Wait there. We don't want to lose sight of that dart!'

Emily Hope slipped on a pair of disposable plastic gloves before carefully picking up the dart.

'Mandy's right,' she announced. 'This dart's been fired recently. I can still smell the chemical preparation.' She showed Sipho and Sandie the traces of blood on the metal point. 'This blood's fresh. I'd say no more than a few hours old.'

'This puts a whole different outlook on things.' Mr Hope's mouth was set in a serious line. 'I think you were right about Leela being too subdued, Sandie. Her dilated pupils and sluggish breathing could be indications that she's been tranquillised. I think we should take a closer look at her.'

Leela was lying in the shade of a tree, sheltering from the intense heat. Her rough pink tongue hung out as she panted to keep cool. Sandie spoke gently to her and coaxed her out into the open with another scrap of meat. Leela seemed reluctant to move at first, but she padded slowly towards her old friend, then flopped on to her belly.

'Good girl. Let's have another look at you, shall we?' Sandie ran gentle hands over Leela's shoulders, then smoothed them down her back. 'Nothing here,' she said. She examined Leela's hindquarters, then gave a small cry as she found what she was looking for on the leopard's right flank. 'Here's the wound from the dart. It looks pretty fresh too.'

Mandy could see the partly-dried blood as Sandie carefully stroked the thick pelt back from the skin.

'I'd better take a look at that wound, just in case it gets infected.' Mr Hope had brought his vet's bag from the Land-rover.

Once again, Sandie soothed Leela with calming words. The leopard stayed calm as Adam snipped away a small patch of fur with sharp scissors. She didn't flinch as he cleaned the wound and even

gave a faint purr as he smeared antiseptic cream on to the bare skin.

It's as if she knows Dad is helping her, Mandy thought.

'That should do it.' Mr Hope stood up and took off his plastic gloves.

'Do we need to give an antidote to the tranquilliser?' Sandie asked. 'There's some in the Land-rover.'

'I don't think so, do you, Emily?' Adam checked with his wife.

Mrs Hope shook her head. 'Most of the effects

of the drug seem to have worn off now. It will only add to Leela's trauma if we give her more medication.'

'Fine. I think she's been through enough for one day.' Sandie sat on the ground with Leela's head resting on her knee. The leopard seemed to have fallen into a relaxed half-doze.

'What I want to know,' James said, 'is who would want to tranquillise Leela?'

'Perhaps whoever did that has taken her cubs?' Mandy suggested.

Sandie nodded. 'It certainly looks that way,' she said, sounding angry.

'Will they have been . . .' James obviously couldn't bring himself to finish his question.

'I doubt they've been killed,' Sipho Ngomane reassured them. He had sunk to the ground and now sat cross-legged on the hard earth.

'But how do you know?' Mandy gave a shudder. 'In India tigers are killed for their fur or for their body parts. They use them in medicine, don't they? Maybe the same thing's happened to Leela's cubs!'

'Hold on a minute, Mandy,' Mrs Hope warned her. 'This is Africa, not India, remember?'

'Your mum's right,' Sandie said. 'Leopards

aren't used in traditional medicine here and if someone was after a leopard pelt, they'd have taken Leela, wouldn't they?'

'Yes, you're right,' Mandy said, following Sandie's reasoning. 'And you can buy leopard skins legally, can't you?' she said, wrinkling her nose with disgust. 'Although I can't think why any sane person would want to!'

Sipho Ngomane nodded. 'I agree. The skin belongs on the leopard. But shooting them is legal in certain parts of South Africa – so whoever drugged Leela was after something else.'

'They wanted the cubs alive?' James sounded puzzled.

'Sandie, you said that oribi, Tasha, had been stolen for a collector,' Mandy said. 'Could the same thing have happened to Leela's cubs?'

'Hmm.' Sandie looked thoughtful. 'There *are* private collectors who will pay for cubs of "exotic" or endangered animals. It might be worth finding out if any more animals have been stolen – because something *very* strange is going on.'

Mr Hope reached inside the Land-rover for more lemonade and handed the drinks round. They all sat silently in the shade while they drank.

Mandy was relieved to think that the cubs were

alive after all, but she remembered Leela's cries of distress. What kind of person would wrench the cubs away from their mother, she wondered. She was determined to do everything in her power to reunite the leopard family.

'Come on,' she said to James, as soon as he had finished his drink.

He looked up, surprised. 'Where are we going?' he asked.

'To look for more clues,' Mandy told him. 'We can start over there, where we found the dart!'

'Hang on, Mandy,' Emily Hope said. 'I think we all need a rest in the shade before we start searching again.'

Mandy shifted her feet impatiently. 'But we haven't got any time to waste!'

Sipho Ngomane stood up, a lanky figure towering over them. He was wearing his khaki shirt, the one with the research base logo on the pocket. That shirt stirred a faint memory in Mandy's brain, but she couldn't quite catch hold of it.

Sipho grinned at Mandy and James. 'I will help you look,' he told them. 'If the thieves have left clues, we'll find them!'

Eight

Mandy and James looked around at the seemingly endless expanse of tough, spiky grass, peppered with low thorny bushes. It seemed an impossible task to search such a vast area.

'Where do we start?' James asked.

'I don't know.' Mandy could see nothing but grass and dry earth.

Sipho Ngomane took one look at their despondent faces and grinned, his teeth very white in his dark narrow face.

'This is Africa, remember,' he said. 'The country is full of secrets. If you learn to understand her, she will yield them. Come on – I'll show you what I mean.'

He led them about two metres to their right and squatted down agilely in a patch of knee-high grass. 'The dart you found was just here, wasn't it?'

Impressed, Mandy and James nodded.

'Look closely. This is the shape your feet made; Mandy's footprints are here, and James's are here.'

Mandy looked down at what seemed to her like undisturbed grass. 'How can you tell?' she asked. 'I can't see anything but grass.'

'It's easy when you know what to look for,' Sipho answered. 'There are different kinds of grass. You must get to know the way it holds different patterns. Some footprints show up pale and some darker coloured. Just as some grass smells sweet and other types smell of salt. You have to learn what to see and smell and hear and then you will understand the grass.'

'Er . . . right.' James sounded intrigued, but doubtful. 'That'll take us about a hundred years!' he whispered to Mandy.

Mandy smiled. James was right. It sounded so complicated.

Sipho threw back his head and laughed at their

gloomy faces. 'Come on. I'll teach you. I'm an experienced tracker. The first thing the trackers of my father's people were taught was to get to know the grass. My father himself taught this to me!'

Then Sipho began his lesson, showing them how to see the grass as he did. He explained what different shadows meant, and invited them to smell and touch the textured blades.

It was a lot to take in and Mandy thought she would never get the hang of it. *Maybe you have to be born in Africa to be able to 'read' the land and plants like Sipho can*, she thought.

Mandy decided to go back to searching the way she knew how. But she winced and straightened up after ten minutes of back-breaking crawling around searching on all fours. 'Who's brilliant idea was this?' she groaned. 'We'll never find anything at this rate.'

She rubbed her nose where sticky grass pollen had brushed on to it. 'Can you see anything, James?'

'No. No luck . . .' James broke off and stared at the ground. 'Hang on! There's something glinting in that grass.'

'Be careful,' Mandy warned him, as he edged

forward. 'It might be another tranquilliser dart.'

'No, I don't think it is.' James was on his knees now, combing through the long grass with delicate fingers, just as Sipho had shown him.

Impressed, Mandy leaned over to watch.

Gradually James uncovered a small object. 'Got it!' He sat up and held out his hand, palm up.

Mandy looked at the piece of shiny metal. It was roughly triangular in shape and scored with deep lines. Along one edge, it was flat and a much lighter colour. 'You did well to find that. Well done!' she said warmly.

James blushed to the roots of his hair. 'I wouldn't have found it if Sipho hadn't shown us how. Look at this broken edge. Looks like a new break. I wonder what this belonged to.'

Mandy experienced a little jolt of recognition. 'I've seen something like this before. I know I have.'

'Where?' James urged her. 'Maybe it's important.'

Mandy shook her head. The memory was just out of reach. 'Maybe I'll remember later on.'

'Found something?' Sipho had appeared by James's side, his feet making no sound on the baked ground.

James held out the piece of metal. 'Mandy thinks she recognises it.'

'Good. Keep hold of it,' Sipho told them. 'You see, you are trackers, like me!'

Mandy beamed at this praise.

'Come with me now. I've found something too.' Sipho led them a short distance away. 'Look.' He pointed to the ground.

Mandy and James saw only flattened grass and a patch of stony red soil – until Sipho showed them the little brownish spots on the grass.

Mandy gasped, feeling her stomach turn over.

'Blood. Is it Leela's or the cubs?'

'I think it was Leela's. This is where she fell down and lay on the ground,' Sipho explained, showing them the faint trails in the grass. 'The dart must have fallen out where you found it. She was getting weaker here, but she still managed to crawl towards her cubs before collapsing.'

'It must have been terrible,' Mandy murmured, her throat tight with emotion. 'Can you imagine lying there helplessly, while someone steals your babies?'

James too looked pale and shocked. He had taken off his glasses and was rubbing at his eyes.

'There's more over here,' Sipho said gently. 'If you don't want to look . . .'

'No. We do. We want to, don't we, James?' Mandy was determined to help.

James nodded and they followed Sipho without speaking. However upsetting it was, Mandy had to see it all, to know everything. She was sure that James felt the same.

'Here, you can see the prints of three men's feet. Just here, two of them kneeled down . . .' Sipho began translating the almost invisible signs. 'Just here, I think there was a wooden crate on the ground. Here are some chips of wood as if the crate was dropped. And look at this.' He opened his hand to show them a scrap of cream-coloured fur. 'Leopard cub.'

Mandy felt furious and sad at the same time. She imagined the men grabbing the cubs, shoving them roughly into a dark, frightening cage, ignoring their cries of distress . . .

She felt the sting of angry tears and blinked them away.

But Sipho still hadn't finished. 'See this patch of earth? Tyre tracks. Special fancy tyres, by the look of them. They belong to a modern jeep.'

Mandy looked up. Three men and a modern jeep. Suddenly the last piece of the jigsaw fell into place for her.

'I know what that piece of metal is!' she exclaimed. 'It belongs to a car mascot – an eagle with spread wings!' The words tumbled over each other in her rush to get them out. 'We saw an eagle mascot on that fancy black jeep in the car park of Letaba House, remember?'

'Wow!' James gasped. 'Yes! I remember it. You were looking at it when that rude man warned us to stay away from his jeep. So it *was* them! I knew there must be a reason why they were so shifty!'

Sipho looked thoughtful. 'They were not

pleased to see us, those men.'

'No, and Sandie didn't trust them either!' Mandy whirled round and looked at Sipho. 'Let's go and tell everyone!'

Sipho nodded. 'I hope we have enough proof. The authorities will not just take our word for it. They will want evidence they can take away.' He smiled. 'They will not see the signs in the grass!'

'Maybe not. But I've got something here that might help.' James dug into the pocket of his shorts and drew out a crumpled piece of paper. He handed it to Sipho. Look!'

As Sipho Ngomane smoothed out the paper a slow smile spread over his face. 'Yes! This is just what we need! Well done, James. You see, you were a tracker before today!'

'What's that?' Mandy asked impatiently.

'The registration number of that jeep,' James told her. 'I was going to tell you that I'd jotted it down, but I must have forgotten.'

'Until now!' Mandy beamed at her best friend. 'James Hunter! Has anyone ever told you that you're absolutely brilliant!'

'. . . and Sipho was so clever, he looked at the grass and worked it all out!' Mandy finished telling the whole story to Sandie and her parents.

'No,' Sipho said modestly. 'You and James found the piece of mascot and James took the jeep's number.'

Sandie was silent for a few moments, as if she was taking everything in. 'It's clear enough what's happened here,' she said. 'We'll have to contact the research base right away. It looks as though the cubs have been taken within the last few hours, so the thieves can't have got far.'

'The radio's in the Land-rover.' Sipho went off to get it.

'Where do you think the cubs are now?' Mandy asked Sandie.

'That's my main concern,' Sandie admitted. 'They could be being held somewhere, perhaps a private game reserve, until their new "owner" can arrange passage for them. But they might already be on their way out of the country.'

'Will the people who took them know how to care for them?' James wanted to know.

'Probably not,' Mr Hope said. 'Looking after such tiny cubs takes patience and specialist knowledge. Two things I doubt these thieves have!'

Mandy was frightened for the poor cubs,

hungry, scared, and missing their mother. Sandie had told her earlier that the cubs could probably survive for a day or so without being suckled. They might still be alive, but they weren't out of danger yet.

Sipho returned with the radio and Sandie tuned it to the frequency for the research base.

'Hello. This is Sandie Howard. This is Sandie Howard. Can anyone hear me?'

A woman's voice crackled back over the transmitter. 'Hello, Sandie. How are you? This is Mmatsatsi Ngomane. Everyone else is over at the hotel for a birthday party. Can I help you?'

'Yes, hi, Mmatsatsi. Please listen carefully. I have some important information. Leela's cubs have been stolen. This is what I need you to do . . .'

The radio crackled as Sandie gave her all the details. Mmatsatsi promised to notify the police and park authorities right away. 'But what are you going to do with Leela?' she asked.

There was a pause while the radio cleared. 'I'm bringing her back to the base,' Sandie said. 'I can't risk leaving her wandering around in distress looking for her cubs.'

'Then you'll need assistance. If you tell me your position, I'll radio the nearest research base and have them send a transporter.' There was another fuzz of static, and a wheezing, whining noise.

'Thanks, Mmatsatsi. That's great.' Sandie gave Mmatsatsi the map reference. 'I'll pass you over to Sipho now. He wants to say hello. I'll contact you again in a few hours, to see if you've come up with anything.'

'OK, Sandie,' Mmatsatsi said. 'Bye for now.'

'Bye.' Sandie handed the radio over to Sipho.

'I don't think the transporter will get here much before nightfall,' she told Adam and Emily Hope. 'And we obviously can't get back to the base while it's dark.'

'No,' Mr Hope agreed. 'We must minimise the stress to Leela as much as possible.'

'So does that mean we'll have to camp out here tonight?' Mandy asked.

'I'm afraid so.' Sandie sounded apologetic. 'I don't want to risk trying to find a trail lodge. We would have to leave Leela here and hope she'd come when I called her in the morning. I'm worried that she'd go wandering off, looking for her cubs during the night. But if we camp here, I'm pretty sure she'll stay close to me.'

'That's fine by us, isn't it, James?' Mandy was delighted at the idea of camping out with Leela.

James nodded and grinned, as if he couldn't think of anything better than having a leopard sleeping next to his tent!

But that wasn't quite what Sandie was planning. She insisted that Mandy, James, and Mr and Mrs Hope should all sleep inside the Land-rover for safety. Only she and Sipho would pitch tents outside and they would take it in turns to keep watch with the rifle close at hand. She was confident that they could trust Leela, Sandie said, but it was well to always remember that 'a leopard is a leopard!'

Sipho cooked a tinned bean and vegetable stew on the small paraffin stove, then fetched some bread from the cool box. It had been a long, tiring day and Mandy ate hungrily. Sandie contacted the base, just before everyone settled down for the night. Paul, Sipho's deputy, was back now and he filled Sandie in on the latest developments.

'Paul says our three men are known to the police,' Sandie told the others. 'One of them, Benjamin Renett, apparently has close links with a wealthy supplier of exotic animals in the United States. They said Renett's a slippery character. They think he's been responsible for a lot of stealing and smuggling of animals within South

Africa's national parks. Paul got the impression that they're very keen to get their hands on him.'

'I know the feeling,' James said grimly.

'Benjamin Renett,' Mandy exclaimed. 'In the carpark at Letaba, we heard one of them call the big, fair-haired man Ben. That must be him.'

She frowned. She still couldn't understand why the smugglers had been particularly nervous around them.

Mandy stared thoughtfully into space. Sipho was sitting opposite, wearing his khaki shirt with the base pocket logo. Her gaze fell on his shirt. Suddenly Mandy realised what she had been trying to remember. 'I've got it! I know why Ben Renett and his friends ran off. It's that shirt Sipho wears, they must have seen the base logo.'

'I think Mandy's right,' her dad said.

Sandie nodded. 'Yes, of course. No wonder the men seemed so nervous around us.' She yawned.

The dusk had given way to darkness and they all settled down to sleep. Despite the cramped conditions inside the Land-rover, Mandy managed to snatch a few hours' rest. She woke early, worrying about the cubs and whether the police would catch Renett and his friends. She desperately hoped they would be able to stop the men who evidently cared only about the money they could make from animals.

Then, in the still morning air, came a heart-rending sound. Leela was calling for her cubs again. Mandy watched through the Land-rover window as Sandie sat on the grass outside her tent, comforting the mother leopard. After a few minutes, Sandie looked up and gestured to Mandy that it was safe to come outside. 'It's OK, Mandy. You can come close. Leela won't mind,' Sandie told her, as she gently opened the door and slipped down on to the hard soil.

Mandy stepped forward and stretched out a hand. Leela purred softly and allowed Mandy to stroke her head. To her delight, the leopard even rubbed her cheek against her palm.

'Thank you,' Mandy breathed, moved almost beyond words that this magnificent animal should want to be friends.

She held her breath, struck once more by the leopard's beauty. Leela's fur was thick and glossy, her golden eyes outlined with pure white. Dark brown rosettes speckled her creamy coat. Mandy could see her special feature, the line of parallel rosettes on her spine.

She spent a few precious minutes speaking softly

to Leela, telling her that it was going to be all right. Mandy was determined they would return Leela's cubs to her. *Oh, please, please, let the cubs be safe*, she wished silently.

She wondered if Leela had passed on her distinctive markings to her cubs – and whether any of them would ever know.

Nine

'Hi!' The driver of the jeep and trailer leaned out of the car window and introduced himself and his companion to Sipho. 'They said at Ubungane that you might need help transporting a leopard. We've got you a trailer and we've brought dart guns with us.'

Mandy saw the men glance at Leela, who was lying on the ground sunning herself about six metres away.

'I thought we'd need to track her before we darted her,' one of them said, looking surprised. 'How come she's so close?'

'This is a special leopard,' Sipho Ngomane told

them. 'She responds to Sandie because Sandie reared her.'

The man nodded, still looking wary. 'OK. Fine. We'll leave the details to you, shall we? Just let us know when you've decided what to do. We'll go and stretch our legs.' The men got out of their jeep and walked off towards the shade of some acacias.

Sandie bit her lip and turned to Emily Hope. 'I'm afraid of Leela's reaction if we shoot her with another dart,' she confided. 'Only a few hours ago someone did the same thing, and her cubs were taken from her. Goodness knows what that's done to her. We need Leela to feel secure and to trust us, otherwise we may get the cubs back only to find that she's rejected them. If we dart her, we may destroy that trust.'

Mandy couldn't help speaking up. 'She's right, Mum. After the last time, Leela will think we're going to do something awful to her.'

'I'm aware of that, love.' Mrs Hope spoke gently, but firmly. 'But Leela will hardly realise what's happening. A moment of discomfort, then she'll be unconscious. She'll wake up safe in her old *boma* at Ubungane base.'

Mandy couldn't help feeling that Leela wouldn't

see it quite like that. All she would know would be a shot, dizziness, more fear, and then she would collapse on the ground in confusion.

'Isn't there another way?' she pleaded. 'Couldn't you give Leela a sedative by injection? That wouldn't upset her so much, would it? And then Sandie could reassure her and lead her into the cage . . .'

'Instead of us having to lift up an unconscious leopard?' Mrs Hope appeared to consider the suggestion, then she shook her head. 'It's just not on, Mandy. It would be far too dangerous to administer a drug by injection. We couldn't guarantee that Leela would keep still and there's the danger of the needle breaking. Who in their right mind would risk giving an injection to a powerful, unpredictable wild leopard . . .'

'I would,' Adam Hope said quietly. 'I think Mandy has a point – although I agree with you in principle, Emily. I'm prepared to give the sedative by injection. Leela was as good as gold when I dressed the wound on her flank. And I trust Sandie to keep her calm while I administer the drug.'

'That's a lot of trust,' Mrs Hope sighed. 'All right, if you're confident enough, Adam. But you'd better have Sipho standing by with his rifle – just in case.'

Sandie gave them both a wide smile. 'Thank you, Adam. Don't worry, Emily. I'll take good care of him.'

'You'd better,' Emily said wryly. 'He's the only husband I've got!'

Mandy let out a sigh of relief. She had complete faith in Sandie's ability to keep the leopard calm.

James, who had been listening, looked puzzled. 'What's the difference between a sedative and a tranquilliser?' he wanted to know.

'They're very similar,' Mr Hope explained, 'but generally a sedative is a weaker dose of a drug, used to calm an animal and make it sleepy, not make it unconscious.'

'Oh, right.' James glanced across at Mandy, who smiled back, glad that Leela was going to be saved the trauma of being darted again.

The two men from the research base helped Sipho to attach their trailer to the back of Sandie's Land-rover. They opened the door before returning to their own vehicle. Sandie was stroking Leela and speaking softly to her. The leopard finally yawned, showing her impressive teeth, then settled down to wash herself.

Mandy, James and Emily Hope watched from inside the Land-rover as Sipho stood nearby with his rifle ready. Mandy held her breath as she saw her father filling a sterile syringe with sedative. He approached Leela slowly, then kneeled beside her and stroked her head. 'Good girl,' he said. 'You remember me, don't you?'

'He's going to give the injection in the loose skin of her neck,' Mandy's mum explained. 'That way, she'll hardly feel it.'

As Sandie spoke soothingly to Leela, Mr Hope bent forward, took a firm grip on the leopard's neck and administered the injection. Apart from a soft growl of surprise, Leela stayed quite still.

Mandy gave a relieved sigh. Emily grinned at her. 'I'm glad that's over! Sandie will have to persuade Leela to get into the cage now before she gets really sleepy.'

'Here they come,' James said.

Sandie began walking towards the trailer, Leela padding along trustingly behind her. The leopard was slow and groggy from the sedative, but Mandy knew that even in this state, a leopard could still be dangerously unpredictable. She strained to see the end of the trailer. Leela reached the ramp and Sandie coaxed Leela to walk up it. At the top of the ramp, Leela hesitated.

Mandy held her breath. Would Leela go into the trailer? She knew animals hated to be cornered. It would be a huge act of trust if she allowed Sandie to lead her into the enclosed space.

'Come on, Leela,' Sandie urged gently. She moved forward out of Mandy's sight, and, after a moment, the leopard followed her into the trailer.

A few moments later, Mandy heard Sandie close the door and slide the bolt.

'Amazing!' James said.

Mandy and James jumped out of the Land-rover and dashed over to where Adam Hope was waiting beside Sipho. Throwing her arms round her dad, Mandy gave him a hug. 'You were great, Dad!'

'Weren't you nervous, Mr Hope?' James asked, looking impressed.

'Me?' Mr Hope grinned, returning Mandy's hug. 'Cool as a cucumber!'

Emily Hope had followed Mandy and James from the Land-rover. Now she kissed her husband on the cheek. 'Well done, Adam,' she said.

*   *   *

'Hello, this is Paul from Ubungane base. I have a message for Sandie Howard. Can you hear me? This is Paul.' The man's voice crackled over the transmitter as they all sat in the Land-rover, ready to set off back to Ubungane research base.

Sandie spoke into the radio. 'Hello, Paul. This is Sandie.'

'Sandie!' Paul said. 'I've got some wonderful news for you. I've just heard that the police have caught Renett and the others trying to smuggle live animals out via an airfield on a private game reserve. They found an oribi, a nyala – and two leopard cubs!'

'What?' Sandie looked as if she could hardly believe it. 'Are the cubs all right?'

Mandy listened nervously.

The transmitter crackled again as Paul replied. 'The police are bringing the cubs straight here. Apparently, we're the nearest research base to the airfield.'

'What condition are the cubs in?' Sandie asked. 'Did they say?'

'No, sorry, Sandie,' he told her. All we know is that they're alive.'

Alive. Mandy could have jumped for joy, but

there was no room inside the Land-rover! James beamed at her. 'Brilliant news, isn't it?'

'How's it going there, Sandie?' Paul's voice asked over the radio. 'Any problems?'

'Everything's fine. We're on our way back with Leela. We should reach Ubungane in about three hours.' There was a whine of static as Sandie finished speaking.

'That's great,' Paul said. 'The cubs should have arrived by the time you get here.'

'I can't wait. Thanks, Paul. Bye for now. See you soon.' Sandie ended the transmission and turned to the others. 'Did you all hear that?'

'Yes. The cubs are safe,' Mrs Hope said. 'That's wonderful news.'

'It's the best news ever!' Mandy agreed, grinning. But her enthusiasm began to fade as she realised that even now the cubs were not safe. They had been without their mother for many long hours, probably kept in a stuffy wooden crate. She knew they must be very weak and traumatised. Mandy just hoped they would survive.

The drive back to the resort felt like the longest of Mandy's life. All she could think about was the cubs. At long last, Ubungane Lodge came into view.

'Look! David, Sophie and Lindiwe have come to meet Leela!' Mandy waved at the figures waiting outside the base.

Mandy and James sprang out of the Land-rover the moment Sipho brought it to a halt. David, Sophie and Lindiwe rushed up, anxious for news. Mandy noticed that, for once, Sophie hadn't got Dilly draped round her neck. *Probably just as well*, she thought. Hyrax was one of the dishes on a leopard's menu!

'The police have found Tasha!' Sophie called joyfully.

But Mandy was more interested in the leopards. 'Have the cubs arrived?' she asked eagerly.

'Yes, just a few minutes ago,' Lindiwe told her. 'Paul's taken them to the medical centre. He's there with them now. We can go and see them if you like.'

Mandy felt torn. She wanted to see Leela safely back in her *boma* but she also felt desperate to see the cubs.

'Sandie's asked your mum and me if we can go straight to the medical centre to help in Levina's absence,' Mandy's dad told her. 'Sandie's going to make sure Leela's settled, then she'll come across to see the cubs. Do you want to come with us?'

'Yes, please,' said James, and Mandy nodded eagerly.

They made their way quickly towards the medical unit with Mr and Mrs Hope leading the way. Paul met them at the door.

'It's good to have you back. I'm pretty sure these cubs are going to need treatment.' He led them into a modern, well-equipped room. 'This is how they arrived,' he said.

Mandy saw a large wooden crate on the floor. There was a sour, stale smell in the air. All she could see through the wooden bars was a tangled bundle of damp spotted fur.

'Oh! This is barbaric,' Mrs Hope said angrily. 'I hope those smugglers get what they deserve!'

'There are heavy fines and prison sentences for smuggling,' Paul told her. 'These thieves won't be stealing any more animals.'

Mandy breathed a sigh of relief. At least the other animals around Ubungane should be safe.

'Let's have this lid off, straight away,' her dad said. 'Give me a hand, would you?' Mr Hope,

James, and Paul removed the heavy lid and leaned it against the wall.

'Oh, the poor things!' Mandy gasped as one of the cubs raised a wobbly head and sniffed at the air. Its fur was flat and dull-looking and the golden eyes seemed glazed with fear.

The other cub had hardly moved. It crouched on the soiled wooden base of the crate, dirty and skinny-looking. The fur around its eyes was matted and sticky and it didn't seem able to open its eyes.

Emily Hope frowned. 'These cubs are in a state of collapse.'

'I doubt they've been given any attention since they were put in that crate.' Mr Hope's mouth was set in a stern line, as he pulled on a pair of disposable rubber gloves. 'Let's get them straight up on to the examination table.'

Mandy felt close to tears as she watched her parents gently lifting the cubs out of the filthy crate. She knew that the cubs were in the best possible hands now, but what if it was too late? James looked white and shocked and Paul was frowning. Mandy couldn't understand how anyone could have let them get into such a terrible state.

'OK. Let's give these two a thorough

examination before we give them any fluids.' Mrs Hope was calm and professional as she laid the smaller of the cubs down gently on the table.

'Just in case we need to anaesthetise them.' Adam Hope nodded in agreement. 'This larger one's a male, by the way. All right, little chap,' he said softly. 'Let's have a good look at you. Would you pass me that thermometer, please, Mandy?'

Mandy watched her dad take the cub's temperature and then check its pulse. 'Hmm. His pulse is steady, but his temperature's up a bit,' he said. 'His airways are clear. No infection there. But see how his ribs are showing, Mandy?'

Mandy nodded. 'He must be starving. He need's Leela's milk,' she said.

'That's right,' her dad agreed. 'But we can't reintroduce the cubs to her yet. We'll need to keep a close eye on them for a couple of days.'

'Will we have to bottle-feed them?' Mandy asked.

Mr Hope nodded. 'I expect you and James can help with that. You've done it often enough.' Mandy looked across at James.

'We'd love to,' he said to Mr Hope.

'All right, little one. You feel very sick, don't

you?' Emily was checking the other cub's ears and mouth.

Mandy moved across to see if her mum needed a hand.

Her mother smiled at her, but her eyes flicked back to the cub, showing concern. 'This one's a girl. She's very dehydrated.'

'How can you tell?' James asked.

Mrs Hope took a fold of the cub's neck skin between gentle fingertips. 'See how loose and sluggish the skin is?' she said. 'In a healthy animal it would spring straight back, but this has hardly any tone. And I don't like the look of that eye infection. I think we'll clean her eyes, then we can get a better look.'

Mandy passed her mum some sterile swabs, and watched while Mrs Hope cleaned the cub's eyes. When the sticky mess was cleaned away, the cub's eyes were still half closed. 'Slip a pair of gloves on, then hold her for me a minute, would you, love?' she asked.

Mandy pulled on the disposable gloves, then took the tiny leopard cub from her mum and cradled it close. It weighed hardly anything, seeming no more than skin and bone. She felt a rush of hot anger against anyone who could do this to an animal, especially one so young and vulnerable.

'You're safe here now,' she whispered, brushing her lips against the top of the cub's head. 'Mum and Dad will make you well again.'

Mrs Hope went to the drug cupboard and came back with a small bottle. She filled a syringe. 'I'm going to give her an antibiotic. That should help clear up the infection.'

The male cub began to mew and struggle as Mr Hope finished his examination. 'He might be weak, but he's still got enough energy to resist being poked about! That's a good sign,' he said. 'He's a lot bigger than his sister, so he probably had reserves of body fat to sustain him. Well – there are no broken bones and no injuries. I think we'll get some fluids into this little chap now.'

Mandy felt heartened by the news. The male cub seemed to have a good chance. But she was really worried about the little female. Mandy stroked the cub's head, but she didn't respond. She just lay on the examination table, her mouth partly open so that Mandy could see the tip of her rough pink tongue.

'Do you think she's going to be all right?' she asked her mum.

Emily Hope gave her a calm, level look. 'I really don't know, love,' she said. 'The next day or so will be crucial.'

Mandy felt a tightness in her chest as she blinked back tears. The little female *had* to get better. She just had to!

Ten

'I'm going to call the male Toto, and the little female Petra,' Sandie declared. She had come straight over to see the cubs as soon as Leela settled into her old home.

'Those are lovely names!' Mandy looked inside the large wire cage where the two cubs were curled up together on clean straw. Toto stirred and yawned sleepily, but Petra was fast asleep. Mandy smiled as the sickly cub gave a soft snore.

'They say sleep is the best medicine,' Adam Hope said. 'There's a lot of truth in that.'

Sandie nodded. 'I don't think I'll be sleeping

much until I know whether these little ones will
survive.'

Mandy looked up at Sandie, glad to know that
someone else felt the same way about the
vulnerable little cubs – she was sure she would lie
awake for hours thinking about the sickly female.
However, that night, after she and James had
visited Leela to make sure she had settled into
her *boma*, she fell fast asleep as soon as her head
hit the pillow. It had been an exhausting couple
of days.

The next morning, Mandy was up and dressed at
first light.

'I'm going over to see Petra and Toto. Are you
coming?' She shook James awake.

He groaned and sat up, fumbling for his glasses.
'OK. Wait for me.'

They found Sipho Ngomane in the medical
unit. 'Hello,' he greeted them, with a smile. 'Have
you come to see the little ones too? I thought I'd
check up on them before I start work.'

Mandy nodded. 'How are they?' she asked
anxiously.

'Come and see for yourselves,' Sipho said,
leading the way.

Toto was awake and looking out of the cage, when Mandy got there. He blinked at her and gave a soft growl. 'Hello. Are you feeling better?' She smiled at him and put her finger in the cage to stroke his soft fur.

Petra was curled up, very still, at the back of the cage. Mandy had a second of panic before she noticed the gentle rise and fall of the cub's breathing. Then the little female stretched and lifted her head. She lay on her side, watching Mandy and James petting Toto.

'Look!' James said excitedly. 'Petra can open her eyes properly now.'

'Oh, yes!' breathed Mandy. 'That's great. And her nose is damp. Yesterday it was dry and hot.' Petra was still weak and less active than Toto, but Mandy felt cheered by the encouraging signs.

They went back to the lodge to give Mandy's parents the good news and found them having breakfast at a table on the outside terrace. 'Hello,' Mr Hope said. 'We came to call for you, but guessed you'd gone to the base.'

Mandy pulled up a chair and sat down. 'Toto is walking round the cage. And Petra's eye infection is miles better!' she reported excitedly.

'Young animals are sometimes stronger than

they look,' her dad said, smiling at the good news. 'I'll check them over later. Sandie will be pleased that they're doing so well.'

'When can the cubs be put in with Leela?' James asked, helping himself from the basket of bread.

'Sandie's the expert on rearing cubs,' Mrs Hope said. 'Why don't you ask her?'

'We will . . .' Mandy was all set to dash straight off to Sandie's lodge, but she saw that James was determined to have breakfast, '. . . after we eat,' she finished with a grin.

Her mum chuckled. 'Lucky it's a buffet breakfast. There's plenty left. Help yourselves.'

'Thanks, Mum!' Mandy piled her plate with fruit and began tucking in. All around the African morning was coming alive. From the veranda she could see brightly-coloured birds flitting through the trees. Realising that the first week of their holiday was almost over, she had a sudden thought. 'When's Levina coming back?' she asked.

'Tomorrow, I think,' Emily Hope replied. 'Maybe the day after. I expect it depends on how well she got on with tagging those roan antelopes.'

'We'll have loads to tell her, won't we?' James mumbled through a mouthful of bread.

'Yes. We've had quite an adventure,' Mandy agreed happily. 'And there's still another two weeks to go!' Mandy couldn't wait to see their friend again. She was looking forward to showing Leela and the cubs to Levina. Maybe the cubs would be back with their mother by then. She crossed her fingers under the table, hoping hard that Toto and Petra would continue to improve.

'Shall we go and find Sandie now?' she asked James when he had finished eating.

'I expect she'll be over at the research base, bottle-feeding the cubs,' Mr Hope said, his eyes sparkling. 'I wonder if she needs any help . . .'

Mandy and James immediately jumped up and headed off to find out. On the way to the base, they met David and Sophie and Lindiwe.

'We're just going to see the cubs, aren't we, James?' Mandy said. 'Shall we all go?'

Sandie looked up and smiled as the little group came into the medical unit. She had two bottles ready and was just lifting Toto out of the cage to feed him. 'Don't crowd the cubs, all of you,' she warned, as they gathered round to look. Then she turned to Mandy. 'Your mum told me that you've bottle-fed young animals before. Would you like to feed Petra?'

'Yes, please!' Mandy breathed. She lifted the little female gently and settled on to a chair with the cub in her lap. Petra blinked up at her and mewed weakly.

'You'll have to encourage her to drink,' Sandie said.

Mandy nodded, beaming at James who was watching closely. She dripped a tiny drop of milk on to her finger and held it to the cub's mouth. Petra poked out her small pink tongue and tasted the milk. Her nose twitched and she reached for the bottle. A few moments later she was feeding happily.

'Well done,' Sandie said. But Mandy hardly heard her, she was so happy to see Petra feeding and on her way back to health.

Later that day, Mandy and James cleaned out the cubs' cage while Mr and Mrs Hope checked the cubs. They were just putting in new straw, when Sandie came into the room. 'Are you sure these are the same two cubs?' she asked, smiling down at Toto and Petra who were exploring an upturned cardboard box on the floor.

'Yes! Definitely the same bundles of trouble!' Mr Hope smiled. 'They've made a remarkable recovery.'

Mandy watched Toto as he crouched down beside the box. Tail lashing back and forth, he began stalking his sister who was out of sight round the other side. Petra made a movement and Toto's big round ears swivelled towards the sound. Suddenly he made a dash for the other cub. He leaped in the air, big clumsy paws ready to ambush her. But Petra darted nimbly to one side and, as he skidded past, swatted him on the side of the head. Toto blinked, sat down, and gave a surprised grunt.

Everyone burst out laughing. 'Petra might be small, but she can look after herself!' James said.

Sandie bent down and picked up Toto. She grinned when the cub gave a growl of protest. 'See the row of tiny parallel rosettes down his spine? Ten – exactly the same as Leela's.'

Toto's markings were very dark and distinct, while Petra's rosettes were a lighter caramel colour. Mandy thought both cubs were beautiful. 'I reckon these two are going to be fine!' she said, picking up Petra and giving her a cuddle. The little cub looked up at Mandy, tilting her small, wedge-shaped head to the side. Her huge rounded ears looked too big for her body. *Ears to grow into*, Mandy thought with a smile.

'I agree.' Sandie gave them a broad smile. 'Toto's fine now, and Petra's much better. You two have helped me make up my mind.'

'You mean – the cubs are ready to go back in with Leela?' Mandy asked excitedly. Sandie nodded.

'That's great!' James exclaimed. 'Can we come and watch?'

'Of course you can,' Sandie said. 'We'd never have found Toto and Petra without your detective work.'

Mandy buried her head in Petra's spotted fur, before she put her into the cage. 'You're going back to your mother where you belong,' she whispered.

'If she'll accept them,' Sandie warned gently. 'We can't be sure.'

Mandy frowned. Surely Leela would accept her cubs? She had been so determined to find them.

At the *boma* they found Leela lying stretched out along her branch. The leopard swung her head towards them, gold eyes watchful and ears alert.

Suddenly she gave a deep growl, whirled around and jumped up higher on to the branch. She crouched there, muscles clenched tight, her tail swinging back and forth.

Mandy and James hung back as Sandie placed the cage containing the cubs beside the high wire fence of Leela's *boma*. Mandy felt nervous. What if Leela didn't accept her cubs back?

Suddenly the cubs began crying hungrily, crawling over each other as they attempted to get to Leela – they had obviously caught her scent.

'This is it,' Mandy whispered to James. 'She's bound to come over when she hears them.'

They watched as the mother leopard sat up and yawned. She climbed slowly and gracefully down from the tree and padded across the grass. Then Leela sat down and yawned again. 'She doesn't seem interested,' James said, sounding disappointed.

Mandy sighed. Leela was washing her face, ignoring the cries of her cubs. She licked her front paw, then curled it round one ear. Had Leela forgotten her cubs so quickly?

Sandie began calling softly to Leela. 'Leela. Come here. Good girl. That's right.'

Leela pricked up her ears and padded over to

the fence near Sandie, who opened the cage and picked up Toto. She held him close to the fence. 'See, Leela? This is your cub. Smell him. Get to know him again.'

Mandy held her breath as Sandie spoke gently and reassuringly, coaxing Leela to take notice of the cubs. *Please accept them back, Leela*, she begged silently.

James looked worried. 'It looks as if there's a problem . . .'

Leela sniffed at the cub. She seemed confused. She had begun to turn away, when, from inside the cage, Petra let out a loud howl of protest. Leela's ears twitched. She turned back, pressed her face to the wire fence and gave Toto a tentative lick.

'I think it's working . . .' Mandy whispered, as Toto now began to wriggle and mew hungrily.

From inside the cage, Petra complained loudly. Leela put her enormous paws on the wire and made a familiar coughing noise that Mandy recognised. 'She's calling to them!' Mandy exclaimed.

Sandie's face broke into a delighted grin. 'Can you bring Petra, please, Mandy?'

Mandy crept forward to help. She carried Petra

to the small food hatch in the side door. Sandie unbolted the secure hatch and put the cubs inside, one by one. At once, Toto and Petra scampered across to their mother. They mewed excitedly and rubbed against her. Leela sniffed them, then began washing them with her rough pink tongue. Minutes later, she lay on her side and the cubs began suckling contentedly.

Mandy stood next to Sandie and watched the wonderful sight. 'Leela looks happy to be a mother again, doesn't she?' she said, turning to James.

He nodded, smiling broadly. 'The cubs will be all right now.'

'Thanks to you two,' Sandie said warmly, 'these cubs will grow up strong and free.'

Mandy felt proud and happy. She watched for a while longer, finding it hard to tear herself away.

'Why did you want to come birdwatching?' James whispered to Mandy.

James, Mandy, and Sandie were in one of the hides overlooking a small waterhole, some way from the resort. It was in a secluded spot within a grove of ironwood and ebony trees, dominated by an impressive rock formation.

Mandy's lips twitched. Poor James. She knew he would far rather be watching Leela and her cubs! 'Sandie said she's got something special to show us,' she said.

'That's right,' Sandie agreed. 'News of a rare sighting came into the base yesterday, just before we put the cubs in with Leela. We should have a good chance of seeing it.'

James nodded. Mandy realised that he was trying to look interested.

Picking up her binoculars, she looked out of one of the narrow slits in the hide. She adjusted the focus and panned up and down the rock face and caught sight of a movement in some bushes near one of the ledges.

Then a sleek black shape stepped into view. She saw the wedge-shaped head and wide-spaced ears, the powerful muscles moving as it padded silently along. She could even see the faint rosettes that spotted the dark pelt. A black panther!

'I can see it!' Mandy managed somehow to control her excitement as she watched the beautiful animal climb the rock face. It glanced towards her and she caught her breath as its pale-green eyes seemed to look straight at her.

James was looking in his bag for his binoculars.

'Oh, no,' he groaned. 'I've forgotten to bring them . . .'

'Never mind,' Sandie said casually. 'Here, you can borrow mine. Look over there at those rocks.'

'Thanks.' James peered through Sandie's binoculars. He fiddled with the focus and then wiped the lenses.

'Hurry up,' Mandy urged him.

James lifted the binoculars. Slowly, he scanned the rock face. 'Oh!' Suddenly he stiffened. 'Look . . . It's a black panther. Wow! It really is! It's fantastic!'

Mandy lowered her binoculars and grinned at Sandie, enjoying James's delighted surprise.

Mandy took a final look. She had one more glimpse of the powerful animal, before it gave a flick of its tail and disappeared out of sight. But she didn't mind. James had seen his black panther. And back at the research base, Leela was waiting with her cubs. That was more than enough for her.

GIRAFFE IN A JAM
Animal Ark in South Africa

Lucy Daniels

A family trip to South Africa means an amazing adventure for Mandy and James. They can't wait to go on safari!

Mandy, James and their friend Levina are watching giraffes at a waterhole when Mandy spots one in trouble. Its legs are splayed to drink and it doesn't seem able to right itself. If the giraffe can't get back on its feet, it will become prey to prowling lions. Levina says they must let nature take its course, but Mandy notices a young giraffe waiting alongside the injured adult. Surely they can't just leave a mother and her baby to die?

Another Hodder Children's book

HIPPO IN A HOLE
Animal Ark in South Africa

Lucy Daniels

A family trip to South Africa means an amazing adventure for Mandy and James. They can't wait to go on safari!

A violent storm causes chaos at the lodge where Mandy and James are staying. When they go outside the resort to check on the damage, they find a mother hippo in distress, standing guard over her trapped calf. The wardens' attempts to rescue the baby hippo fail when their jeep gets stuck in the mud. But if they don't free the baby soon, he and his mother will die. Can Mandy help the hippos?